By Joan O'Hagan

A ROMAN DEATH
AGAINST THE GRAIN
DEATH AND A MADONNA
INCLINE AND FALL

A ROMAN DEATH

A ROMAN DEATH

JOAN O'HAGAN

A CRIME CLUB BOOK
DOUBLEDAY
NEW YORK LONDON TORONTO SYDNEY AUCKLAND

All of the characters in this book are fictitious,
and any resemblance to actual persons, living or
dead, is purely coincidental.

A Crime Club Book
Published by Doubleday, a division of
Bantam Doubleday Dell Publishing Group, Inc.
666 Fifth Avenue, New York, New York 10103

Doubleday and the portrayal of a man
with a gun are trademarks of
Doubleday, a division of Bantam Doubleday Dell
Publishing Group, Inc.

Library of Congress Cataloging-in-Publication Data
O'Hagan, Joan.
A Roman death / Joan O'Hagan.
p.   cm.
"A Crime Club book."
ISBN 0-385-24988-8
I. Title.
PR9619.3.038R66   1989
823—dc19

First Edition in the United States of America, 1989

To the Reader

The events told in this book took place in Rome almost two thousand years ago when Julius Caesar, soon to be assassinated, was at the summit of his power. The book lifts a curtain on a world very different from ours: supremely civilised in some respects, barbaric still in others; a world where superstition, magic and slavery coexisted with a complex system of law, logic and administrative efficiency. But despite the well-developed legal system, Roman criminal law had nothing resembling a police force to back it up. The injured party—or his family if he were dead—provided the prosecution at a trial, and the outcome usually depended, as you will read, more on the oratorical powers and persuasiveness of the opposing counsel than on objective sifting of evidence. But in those days too the stakes were high when murder was the charge and those involved feared and hoped and suffered just as you would, should fate tomorrow cast you in their role.

The women of Republican times are silent. Rarely calling for comment in the history books, they are named on tombstones, flit in arrogant beauty through poetry, as Lesbia did, or even perhaps as a monster of iniquity in a court of law, as with Sassia from Larinum. But they themselves do not speak and they have left no literature of any sort of their own. In this book, however, Roman women live and love and hate anything but silently.

Further Note for the Reader

ROMAN NAMES: Women used only the feminine form of the family name, so that Quintus Fufidius' daughter was called simply Fufidia.

MARRIAGE: Roman women had a real degree of freedom, being able to own property. But both before and after marriage a woman was always in the legal power of some man.

There were two sorts of marriage:

"Free" marriage, where a woman remained in her father's power after marriage and could inherit from him independently of her husband;

"Manus" marriage, where the woman passed into the *manus* (or hand) of her husband, leaving the family of her birth and becoming part of that of her husband. In contrast with a "free" marriage, she was in the legal power of her husband. She could possess no property of her own. Everything was vested in her husband or in her husband's father. Anything that came to her by gift or bequest or in any other way during the marriage was absorbed into her husband's property.

CARNIFEX: Executioner or hangman.

AEDILE: Magistrate who superintended public works, buildings and shows.

PRAETOR: Magistrate charged with administration of justice.

PROPRAETOR: After a year as praetor, one who is sent to govern a province.

CINAEDUS: A wanton or shameless person.

Those readers who would like to know more about life in the Rome of Helvia and Fufidius might turn to *Catullus and His World* by T. P. Wiseman, Cambridge University Press, 1985.

A ROMAN DEATH

I

On a late August day of the year 45 B.C., in her villa on the Esquiline, Helvia, wife to Quintus Fufidius, sat straight on her high-backed hard chair looking at the Roman senator's wife who had requested the honour to call on her. Servia sat even straighter and far less comfortably. Helvia, who disliked her, had studiously offered a resplendent seat of marble only recently imported from Paros. Upon the thinnest of cushions, Servia would soon be suffering acutely. The woman's daughter and son, ten- or eleven-year-olds, had accompanied her. Her escort of slaves sat meekly by in a row. Helvia's own slaves came and went, offering refreshment.

They had sighed about the heat—terrible, all day—and complimented each other on the material of their dresses, on their ornaments. They had discussed property prices and the difficulties and expenses of life in Rome, though the conversation carefully excluded political sympathies. Who knew what informers might be present even in this domestic gathering?

"You will be in town for the triumph, of course?" asked Helvia politely. She moved restlessly, all her own slim blond elegance recoiling at the plump and over-bejewelled swarthiness of the other.

"I told the children they must not expect the same magnificence as last year after Caesar's victory at Thapsus. Yes, Publius? You may speak."

The boy bowed his head and then raised piercing black eyes to his mother and Helvia.

"We're to have seats on the Clivus Capitolinus. We'll see the captives before they are strangled," he said with relish. "And we will see Caesar laying his laurel branch and wreaths in the lap of Jupiter. And the sacrifice of the victims."

"Yes, we will see the booty and the captives in chains, and the oxen, the white oxen,'' gurgled his younger sister. "And Caesar too. His face painted all red, and with his gold oak-leaf crown."

"Do you know that the crown is held over him by a slave?" asked Helvia kindly. "And the slave whispers to Caesar that yet he is mortal? 'Look behind you,' he says to Caesar, 'and remember that you are a man.'"

The child's eyes dulled for a moment, then sparkled again as she cried, "I want to see the prisoners. I want to see them strangled!"

"You can't," said her brother. "They do them down in the Tullianum where we can't go."

"That will do, Sextilia. They get so excited," said the woman to Helvia. "Particularly Sextilia."

"What a perfect little darling Sextilia is," returned Helvia blandly, regarding the child and inwardly wondering if she tortured her dolls.

"Oh, Mamma," broke in the boy, with an affected gesture of dismay. "What if Caesar has not killed enough men, Mamma? And they can't have the triumph at all!"

"There, there, I'm sure he has killed enough," said his mother consolingly.

"I imagine," said Helvia drily, "Caesar will have had no difficulty in bringing the numbers up to the five thousand dead requisite for a triumph. It is five thousand, isn't it, Publius? I'm sure you are well informed on the subject."

The eyes of the two women met in momentary amity, each aware of the ominous rumblings of anger in Rome at this triumph over a fellow Roman, eldest son of Pompeius Magnus, who had been one of the very greatest of them all. They would watch the triumph, of course, from the protection of the covered stands put up for the well-born and the wealthy, secure above the surging crowds of the common people, who would think only of gorging themselves on the handouts of feast food and the gladiatorial blood to come. But whatever they thought, all present would be infected by the same hysteria, and great induced roars of praise for Caesar would seem to split open the very sky.

"Caesar can ride a horse at full gallop with his hands behind his back," the little girl babbled excitedly. "And he writes letters while he rides!"

"Dictates letters," her brother corrected her patronisingly.

"Caesar never sleeps!" shouted Sextilia.

Servia gave her tinkling laugh and waved fingers heavy with precious rings.

"I took the children to see the new temple Caesar has consecrated to Venus Genetrix." She dropped her voice and leaned close to Helvia. "It is something new for Rome, isn't it, for a harlot to share the honours with the goddess?" She whispered now, "All gilded, she is."

"She means Cleopatra!" cried her son. "Of course she means Cleopatra! Oh!" The boy clapped a hand to his mouth and laughed roguishly at his mother, who shook her head at him indulgently.

But her incorrigible son sprang to his feet, rolling his eyes and chanting:

> "O Roman men, for your own sake
> Lock up your wives! A bald old rake
> Has stuffed your gold 'tween Gaulish thighs
> And he'd have yours before he dies!"

The ribald jingles that, by immemorial right, a victorious army bawled out about their general in a triumphal procession would not be any the less ribald about Caesar, who would be sure to have some of his women and boys following him in special carriages. "Every woman's husband and every man's wife," one old senator had sourly called him.

"Publius! No more!" cried his mother. She turned once more to Helvia.

"You have been in Pompeii, I hear. You travel so much. You have the advantage over me. Of course, you were born in the Transpadane, that—er, little outpost of empire."

Helvia smiled, waiting.

"Your family, of course, have far-reaching connections, I am told."

Helvia bowed silently. She knew this was a sneering reference to her family's export of wine and Arretine pottery to Narbonese Gaul.

"I hope," continued Servia, "you had a sufficient escort on your journey."

"I came by ship and reached Rome only yesterday. I found a convenient vessel owned by a friend of my husband." Helvia tilted her head in annoyance. "I went by litter to the port at Pompeii," she added carefully. "The entire family of my aunt put me on board. My freedman conducted me from Ostia."

"You had a smooth passage?"

Helvia assented.

"My travel on water has been confined to processions on the Lacus Nemorensis to the temple of Diana."

"I like the sea."

"I would never have been permitted to travel alone. Of course, you will be used to great freedom in the Transpadane."

"My father was strict enough!"

Helvia thought of her father's estate in the northern Italian town of Brixia, that old stronghold of the Cenomani, now something more than a Roman garrison town, of the town square with its pillared portico, filled with businessmen, soldiers on furlough, peasants and tradespeople. There was a vigour and freedom beyond the narrow sense implied by this woman. Helvia looked at and through her. She had spent much time on the deck of the freighter which bore her from Pompeii, feeling the sea move under the thin wooden shell, hearing again the creaking wood and the rush of wind. She thought of the waters of Lake Benacus up north, now dancing under the sunlight, now furious under the pageant of racing grey clouds, of Gaius Catullus' little house on Sirmio, of the yacht which her brother had kept there. That had been freedom for her, yes—of a real sort.

The other woman was talking now of her brother, who had recently finished a term of official duty in Delos.

"The townspeople wished to honour him after his quaestorship and they forced—yes, simply forced on him—a statue. He is represented, I think, as Hermes—with his own head, of course. Moreover, they insisted on portraying his wife and the children as well. Can you guess what they were represented as?"

"His wife was Aphrodite, I expect. I hope that the children, in this case, escaped bisexuality."

Servia said acidly, "They were Loves. I suppose you have little in the way of statues in Brixia."

"My family is not of Gallic stock, you know! And Brixia is as

Roman as we can make it." Helvia became rather pink in the cheeks.

She did not mention her father's library, of notable quality, nor the excellent Greek education which he had decreed for his children, even for his daughter; nor the exquisite intricacy of her brother's poetry, the genius and passion of poetic outpouring of his friend Catullus, who came from nearby Verona, the many friends and acquaintances of culture—which meant, of course, Greek culture—who might end up in Rome, but who hailed from the far provinces such as these lands "this side of the Alps" and "beyond the Po."

Servia, however, had come now to the real purpose of her visit, broaching it in indirect fashion.

"Your husband was not able to accompany you to Pompeii?"

"He has been on business up in Gaul, for the town of Arpinum. He returns very soon."

"Your children, then, are staying at your summer villa in Tusculum?"

"My son Quintus is in Greece. Fufidia is in Tusculum, where her aunt has charge of her."

"Ah! Then it was Fufidia I saw on the day of the Vinalia walking unattended by servants in the town!"

"It's not possible. She would certainly not have been allowed by her aunt—or by the servants—to wander off like that."

The woman nodded.

"I'm glad to hear it, though I was sure it was your daughter. Some other girl, no doubt. There was dancing, you know. The girl was dancing as well. A big crowd. You know what happens on such an occasion. I only mention it because, if it had been your daughter, I thought you should know. The girl was dressed in quite expensive clothes."

"It could not possibly have been Fufidia?" Helvia was angry, regarding the enamelled eyes, smarting at the scarcely veiled insult.

As she got up to go, Servia launched her parting shot.

"I *am* relieved. The girl was with a young man who made very free with her, by all accounts." She laughed, and coming close to Helvia, raised a hand quickly to remove a hair—real or imagined—from Helvia's shoulder. Flicking it away, she laughed.

"But now I can leave, assured that my fears were quite unfounded."

Helvia's heart missed a beat. Fufidia, at fourteen years, was between a child and a young woman—but very much a child still. She had seen her a month before disciplining her dolls, sitting—a grave little figure of justice as she put words of guilt into the mouth of one, stern retribution into that of the other. Grave, childish, so charming.

Servia departed with her young in the closed litter allowed to wives of senators.

"Not that I enjoyed travelling here," she proclaimed loudly as she got in. "To pass through the Subura leaves one breathless with disgust. It isn't good for a girl to see a half-naked prostitute, as I'm sure little Sextilia did. Then we were held up by a wretched slave carrying his gibbet on the way to execution. There was quite a procession after him, near the Esquiline Gate, and we had to wait till it passed. I drew the curtains of course. I don't enjoy such sights. The *carnifices* were goading him on and he was screaming dreadfully. You can hardly get through the streets sometimes."

Grumbling loudly, she made her exit at last.

She had done her work well. Helvia paced the floor, miserably worried, her thoughts wholly on her beloved daughter. Could it really have been Fufidia in a street in Tusculum together with a young man? Impossible. Helvia had left her in Gratidia's care and the villa in Tusculum was well staffed with reliable slaves. Servia must have been sure of her story, all the same. She would not otherwise have dared to impute such disgraceful behaviour. And this could ruin plans that Helvia and her brother Cinna had for the betrothal of Fufidia to that most desirable young man Gnaeus Plancius, son of a senator from Atina, of good solid equestrian descent like themselves, gifted and prosperous. And more than anything, dependable, a husband with whom her daughter would be assured—even in these troubled times—of a pleasant and secure life.

II

On the day of the Vinalia the previous week, August storm clouds had mounted steadily over Latium. Great Rome had sweated. Even up in the Alban hills, among the old oaks and chestnuts, rich owners of summer villas breathed an air that was scarcely cooler.

Fufidius had built his villa high up in Tusculum. From the terrace the land dropped sharply away and in mid-afternoon his daughter sat on the wall looking down on an expanse of turquoise wooded country, endless and shimmering like the sea. The walled garden was shrouded by tall trees, enlivened and refreshed by the pride of Fufidius—cascades, formed by his private tapping of the Aqua Crabra and now plashing on two levels into a deep stone basin. Earlier, his daughter Fufidia had slipped off her robe and plunged into the delicious waters of the basin, under the gaze of a piteous-eyed and shaggy marble Pan. She had let the cascade slip down her naked body and had sung in delight at its silken caress of the new roundness of her breasts and its cool engulfing of her belly and thighs. She knew no one else would see her. Aunt Gratidia was still sunken in the torpor of a wine-enhanced siesta and the slaves had gratefully taken their rest. Both her parents were away. She felt restless, for at fourteen a girl does not notice the weather, and rarely feels tired.

Still more girl than woman, Fufidia was charming, with a mane of silken blond hair, evidence of a distant Celtic ancestor, and happy blue eyes. Now she slid down from the wall and stood quite still on the mosaic pavement of the terrace. From above, up in the town, came the notes of an orchestra. Fufidia placed her feet carefully on two petals of a mosaic flower and began to weave a dance—a dance with little movement of her feet, though otherwise of a nature which could only be called suggestive. She was of course forbidden to dance like that. She had learned the movements from a slave who had once been a dancer and who could also be bribed to bring her Greek tales. From that distance the music came down thin and lingering and disturbing. Fufidia knew the town square was ablaze with flowers, carefully arranged by the peasants in a floral carpet to spell out the names of the gods whose festival it was that day. Jupiter, of course, but also Venus, who had somehow wormed her way into the Vinalia *festa,* nobody quite knew how. It was well before the time when the grapes would be gathered and pressed, but Jupiter's priest presided at prayers to see them safely through this vital ripening period. A snowy white lamb would be sacrificed and the priest would cut out the entrails. He would pick a bunch of grapes and offer them as well to the god.

Tired of solitary dancing, Fufidia went to the wall and drew from a secret cache two rolls of papyrus and settled down to unroll her favourite. *Erotic Tales of Chaereas and Callirrhoe* was her latest and best toy, with the added fillip that it was illicit. Unrolling the papyrus by a third, she read aloud so as to prolong the pleasure: "Dionysius could not get to sleep. His whole being was in Aphrodite's shrine; he could recall every detail—her face, her hair, the way she turned, the way she looked at him . . . desire flooded over him . . ."

Fufidia wriggled pleasurably, then impatiently unrolled the whole scroll to the end—not an easy task—and read aloud, slowly:

"They were like people plunged in a deep well who can barely hear a voice from above. Slowly they recovered their senses; then they saw each other and embraced each other passionately—and fainted again, a second and a third time. They could say only one thing: 'You are in my arms—if you really are Callirrhoe, if you really are Chaereas!' "

So it ended happily. She might have known it. Fire, but a chaste fire, crept down her innermost parts, down her marrow. She had no name for this heavenly world of the written romance. She had led a staid existence, and Callirrhoe was far removed from the reality of a Fufidius' daughter of the present age.

Without warning an apple thudded gently down into her lap. Fufidia sat like a stone. A voice said from above, *"Salve!"*

Guiltily, she grasped the roll, rewinding it as fast as she could. Robust laughter, a young man's laughter, sounded, and turning round she beheld Chaereas himself spring down from the wall, landing at her feet.

She said the first thing that came into her head. "Aunt Gratidia is asleep." There was panic in her tone.

"You're in my arms—if you really are Callirrhoe!" he mimed, with a winning smile.

She sprang up and drew herself up haughtily in imitation of her mother. Then she turned to go.

Lucius Scaurus watched her walk slowly away towards the house with her flowing stride. He grinned. The garden shimmered in the heat. The sweat ran down his legs. A cursed hot sun today, even up here in Tusculum, rivalling North Africa. And, with the thought of Africa, there came flooding back the dreadful memory of dead men in their thousands lying sun-bloated and mutilated after battle, as he'd seen them in Greece —as they'd lain there after Thapsus. He congratulated himself once more on getting out of Africa alive.

He took a sudden decision, then, and ran after the girl. He couldn't know, as he ran, that he had taken the first step on a course that would mark him for death—sure and relentless as any on the battlefield.

He caught her up just as she got to the portico, and gently grasped her shoulder.

"Don't go," he breathed.

She looked up into smiling eyes that seemed to have absorbed the colour and warmth of the summer day, grey-blue eyes, black-lashed, in a tanned sensitive face. She noticed his curly black hair and how proudly he held his head. As beautiful as a god. She had no idea of the interested assessment being made of her.

"Who are you?" she asked.

"Can you ask? I am Chaereas! It is the feast of Venus, and she has revealed me to you."

Fufidia objected. "You are Roman."

"Well, actually I am your neighbour, but today I'm Chaereas.

The fun will begin soon up in the town. Come and see it with me!"

Fufidia's eyes swivelled to right and to left. She was totally unprepared, her education not having included such things.

"There'll be dancing," Lucius Scaurus added, watching her. "Only for a little while. No one will know."

Her eyes, beautiful and candid, assented. Behind lay a sweet passiveness, a simple mind open to impressions. A young girl of some rank had no need of great intelligence. And with that beauty . . .

Up in the town there was a rollicking excitement. As they mingled with the crowd he caught her hand, and his fingers stroked her palm. Fufidia—or was she Callirrhoe?—felt wave upon wave of hot excitement flood through her. Lucius chose not to say that only a little while before he had seen her as a nude virgin innocently enjoy the waters of the fountain and mimic the lewd movements of a prostitute-dancer, but he said, "Dance for me now."

He led her into the porticoed square, lined with shops, before the little theatre with its curving rows of stone seats. Country folk were treading the pavement in the strict rhythms of their ancient forebears.

"You know I can't in public!" Fufidia gasped.

He drew her to him, however, and she danced.

The day was the nineteenth of August or, by the reformed Julian calendar, XIV Kal. Sept. The hills were powerful, brooding, malignant. Up in his temple on the summit of the Alban Mount the all-powerful Jupiter Latiaris brooded, perhaps still enraged— for his memory is infinite—at Rome's subjection of the ancient league of Latin cities, an act itself lost in the depths of time for ordinary mortals. Or, perhaps again, in his own festival that year he had detected a flaw in the rites. In the bloody times of civil war, hardly over, did the god require more than the pure white heifer that had never known the yoke? Humans had once been sacrificed at his altar, as the *oscilla* or little puppets fashioned like human beings bore witness, dangling from the trees.

Fufidia and Lucius were still in the town square when a tremendous crack of thunder burst on them. Lightning streaked simultaneously across the sky. The whole world seemed on fire and the thunder rolled and crashed ominously.

"In an hour they'll have the bonfire," commented Lucius, regarding the girl's perfect profile.

But just at that moment Jupiter's sky opened and in an instant the whole world was awash, flooded and battered by a deluge of godlike proportions.

"Come!" shouted the young man.

He flung his arm round her and as they ran she just heard the words, "I know a place where we can go afterwards."

"Oh, the bedcovers!" Fufidia cried in dismay as they rushed to the shelter of the portico.

From all the little balconies round about heavily embroidered bedcovers—family treasures through generations—had been displayed that morning and now, in a flash, all hung sodden and perhaps ruined.

"You've spoilt your best gown." He fingered it. "It's like silk . . . beautiful."

Fufidia shrugged. "I have others, better than this."

"This is a very fine one. And it comes from far away."

"From Kos. It is very like silk, Mamma says. They weave it there."

"Does your father deal in them?"

She stared. "Deal in them? No. He buys them for me."

An explosion of godlike power deafened them and the earth shook. Fufidia screamed. All around was uproar.

"Don't worry. Only a little earth tremor." And the thunder banged. A comforting, strong arm crept around her waist and his head bent over her. She saw an aquiline nose and full-lipped mouth. She panicked, struggled, and his lips brushed hers. For a second the childhood precepts she had so laboriously written on her slate and woven into her samplers on virtuous behaviour in women struggled once more with the surge of emotion she had felt when chancing on the couplings of peasant or slave. Then the boy's hot breath, the sweet salty tang of his young flesh, overcame her. It was the moment Fufidia had, hitherto, lived for and her lips sought his.

"Perbaccho," he panted, minutes later. "It's very . . . good to kiss you."

He pushed them apart gently. It was getting very crowded in the portico. Bodies jostled them.

"That dress," Lucius said suddenly. "Your father imports them for you."

"Yes, I told you." She looked at him in surprise.

His eyes were on the precious bracelets on her arms and neck. They were the finest specimens of the goldsmith's art.

"Your father is a rich man."

"I don't know. He has three villas. As well as farms. And I hear him talk of the loans he makes."

"And have you a sister as pretty as you?"

"A sister? Oh no. I have only a brother."

The young man's eyes were thoughtful now.

"How big is your villa here?"

"Not big like yours." Fufidia had heard sounds of revelry one night from the next villa and seen the grounds bright with lamps. "Ours is little really. Only two *iugera*. But my father always says, 'Buy a modest one if you must, as long as it is in the best part and the richest street!'"

Lucius laughed wryly. Inside, the splendid villa of the Scauri next door was largely an empty shell, stripped of its riches.

"The rain has stopped for the moment," he observed. "We'd better get away while we can."

Jupiter, obviously, had not finished with them yet. Thunder still rumbled and the sky was black. Lucius hurried Fufidia back to her villa. Once there, he caught her to him again. But it was a very brief kiss and immediately he was gone.

It had been delightful to play with this innocent girl but today was crucial for him. His father had insisted that they reach a decision on his future before leaving for Rome the following day. The two of them had come to Tusculum to arrange for necessary repairs to the villa, which, it was hoped, would soon sell for a good price.

Money, or rather the lack of it, was the problem. Lucius thought moodily how unpleasant it was to be short of funds when there were so many things to do in Rome, but his father could afford to give him only a miserable allowance. And then there were his gambling debts, which his father didn't know about, while creditors were getting every day more insistent.

His family was of course one of the great names, having provided a consul some sixty years before. His own father had been
propraetor in Sardinia and aedile in Rome. Why had he been so
stupid in throwing his money around, plundering the family estates? Grandiose villas, shows of unsurpassed magnificence and
now near-penury. His mother Mucia had been more sensible.
She had left his father once his money was running out and
married Pompeius, but had hedged her bets by also becoming
one of the mistresses of his rival Caesar, remaining to this day in
Caesar's favour. But she wasn't a source of income.

His father had been brutally frank. "You will marry money,
there is no other quick alternative. I don't have any left. And
with the name of Aemilius Scaurus, you're a good catch. What
woman wouldn't like to have such a handsome young husband—
and one due to go off again to the wars." But his father hadn't
only talked. He had estimated the wealth of a number of women
and made discreet enquiries into their availability. Finally, he
had settled on Julia as the best prospect.

"But she's forty if she's a day and I'm only twenty-two," Lucius had objected.

"Not the point. You don't have to be faithful, you fool. She's
very rich, the sole beneficiary of a husband who put together a
tidy fortune in the East—and then conveniently died. And she
isn't very fit. That's a decided point in her favour. We could well
have her estates within five years."

But now, as he waited for his father to be free from discussions with builders, Lucius' mind was replacing rich Julia with
the pretty girl he had just been with. The dowry her family could
provide her with would surely not be less than Julia's money.
And in her leggy slimness, almost that of a boy, Fufidia wouldn't
repel him in the necessary conceiving of sons as would the mature and insistent sexuality of a Julia.

III

Fufidia's father was coming home by stages after months away in Cisalpine Gaul. He had taken ship from Genua and put in at Caieta, forty Roman miles down the coast from Circaeum. He had with him the bags containing the large sums of money resulting from the property transactions and loan repayments which he had undertaken on behalf of a group of Arpinum citizens as well as some Roman property owners. He saw to the unloading of his baggage and settled his account with the ship's master, with whom he had driven his customary hard bargain. Lastly, he gave out the necessary tips with a careful hand.

"Fufidius' purse is most skillfully made," a friend once commented. "Coins that go in so easily come out so slowly."

Together with the two other knights who had accompanied him and their ten-strong escort, he travelled along the river valley of the Liris and climbed up to Arpinum at the magic golden hour of sunset when life slowed and relaxed. They wound up through an ageless pattern of little fields of corn and olives and vines. In the town people strolled in the forum and the taverns were busy. At the sight of his litter, strung between two mules, and the small procession that followed, people hailed Fufidius from all sides and he felt the warm glow of homecoming.

Wealthy man of affairs in Rome now, and owner of numerous farms as he was, Fufidius was still an Arpinum man at heart. He had settled in Rome to give his son an urban education—pure Latin and the best of practical training in law. But it was in these parts that he had been born and reared, and this narrow main street, widening out into the forum round which the public buildings clustered, was one of his first memories. A fine little hill town on its two spurs. Up above was the centuries-old citadel of the ancient Volscian people.

They were a sturdy lot in Arpinum. The town had received

the Roman citizenship one and a half centuries before. It had produced the great soldier Gaius Marius, who had saved Italy from the Cimbrian hordes, and after him, from the ranks of its local families of rich landowners, Arpinum had sent many praetors and consuls to Rome. It had also produced Cicero, now renowned throughout the Roman world as statesman, orator and writer.

Fufidius stayed that night and the following two nights in the house where he was born: a small place once, now much extended. Then the third morning he went down and joined the Via Latina, oldest of all Roman roads, at the seventy-ninth milestone from Rome, and travelled to Tusculum, where he expected to find his wife Helvia and his daughter.

"I get back to Tusculum after months away and Helvia is still in the south, you are asleep, not a slave in the whole place and then I find Fufa coming in unaccompanied from the street!"

Fufidius looked angrily at Gratidia. "You know Fufidia mustn't be allowed out alone. It's not the thing at all, as you know very well. And it's not safe, even up here."

He did not utter the words that welled up hotly inside him— that Gratidia had drunk too much again and had slept for hours. A shameful thing in a woman—better hidden, better never admitted even in private.

"Her lessons . . . ?" he continued out loud.

"There are the summer *festa,"* Gratidia protested. "The Vinalia only a few days ago. And today the slaves have gone to some festivities up in the town . . ."

"Any excuse will do," he grumbled. "And only a day or two ago all the women went off to the Lacus Nemorensis, I suppose, with their interminable votive offerings. Disgusting some of them, too. Bits of their insides. The goddess Diana must be overjoyed."

"You shouldn't speak so insultingly. Of Diana, too."

"What's Fufidia do with herself up here?" he asked.

"She has her lessons with Sositheus. She can say her Ennius off very prettily."

Fufidius mumbled something and was silent. He looked at the old woman he referred to as his aunt. She was in her sixties, with a thick tough body, and a strong-featured face with brown intelligent eyes. She had a will of iron, this distantly related aristocrat with her driving ambition for the family—*his* family, ever since her own had nearly all perished years before in Sulla's proscriptions.

"Fufa is now a young woman. At fourteen she may well be engaged. I was engaged at twelve."

"Yes, yes. I've heard you say so before." Fufidius moved impatiently. "I don't want Fufa to wander off like that again," he said sternly. "I have business now in Aricia. I suppose I can find someone to drive me there. Unless all the drivers are getting drunk, too."

Gratidia knew she had been at fault. She said, now, with cunning, "I should think Marcus Junius Brutus treated your delegation well after that handsome letter Cicero wrote about you."

She purred as she said it. A Gratidia had married Cicero's great-grandfather. *She* remembered—and fostered—the connection. Through her intervention, Fufidius had spent a year as military tribune in Cilicia with Cicero when Cicero went out there as governor.

"You talked with Marcus Brutus?"

"Only very briefly when we were presented to him."

"Cicero praises you in the letters. You know he said you share in his literary pursuits. A nice way to put it. He told me you are an orator *manqué.*"

Fufidius laughed, in his deep voice, and took a turn about the room. Gratidia knew what pleased him. She knew his profound admiration for Cicero.

"Vale, mi fili."

She watched him stride vigorously off. He was tall and moved with a natural grace. His dark and lively eyes set off the clear ivory of his skin. His laugh was good to hear—still boyish and unrestrained in his thirty-ninth year. How attractive he must be to any woman, Gratidia thought. And his growing wealth gained the respect of men.

But Fufidius did not leave Tusculum just then. Scarcely had he finished talking to Gratidia when a servant appeared from the villa next door with a message which made Fufidius immediately change his plans. The servant of Marcus Aemilius Scaurus had to repeat the message before Fufidius absorbed it. His master wished Fufidius to dine that day if convenient. Fufidius sat down abruptly.

"He wants me to dine?"

The man said, for the third time, "If it is convenient."

"Yes, well. Of course. Tell him yes."

Fufidius would have expected Scaurus to want to see him soon. Up in Gaul he had done some business on his behalf and he would have reported on it before too long. But a Fufidius would rarely be called on to dine with a Scaurus. He had never had such an invitation before from a patrician, descended from the earliest aristocracy of Rome.

Fufidius bathed and had himself anointed. Soon after the middle afternoon, clad in his best toga, he crossed the hot tiles of the courtyard next door. To his surprise, the garden wilted unkempt in the heat and there were few servants around. However, Scaurus was his usual impressive figure. A big man in his mid-fifties, with all the attitudes of nobility and power. A still handsome strong face, with deep cleft lines on forehead and a hard humorous mouth, a grim line running each side of it from nose to lip. He limped a little as he came to receive Fufidius. Gout, he said. The most surprising thing of all was that no other guest was present. Scaurus' freedman and secretary appeared briefly for orders, but the two men then settled down to eat alone. Fufidius lay propped on one elbow, straining to appear at ease.

The food was simple but good, and when the main course was served, Fufidius said, truthfully, that he had rarely tasted such deliciously flavoured chicken.

"The sumptuary law doesn't make entertaining any easier," grumbled his host, "but it is all our own produce up here. And we have a good wine."

It was indeed a good wine—Falernian of a famous year—that they drank. Scaurus drank deeply and from politeness Fufidius felt obliged to do the same. Drink helped the gout, Scaurus explained, indicating his bandaged foot.

"Such wine can do only good," remarked Fufidius politely. He was delighted to be the recipient of such largesse.

After he had been given a full account of his property up in

Gaul, Scaurus said, a sneer tingeing the compliment, "You've built yourself a fine house next door. Will you manage to hang on to it?"

"Private holdings have not been appropriated for Caesar's veterans up till now," Fufidius said cautiously. "Caesar is merciful."

"Oh, Caesar is generosity itself, of course," interrupted Scaurus contemptuously. "Generous and merciful as victor. Let us never forget it! At a price that fills his coffers and makes us all paupers." He drank. "These are sad times. One hears talk that he plans to remain dictator for ten years. The Senate might have coped with Pompeius now, had he been spared."

Yes, you mean they'd have got the better of him, thought Fufidius.

Scaurus had been Pompeius' friend.

"My sons thought Pompeius was another Alexander," Scaurus said, watching Fufidius for any sign of dissent. But there was none. Fufidius, too, would have preferred Pompeius, the upholder of their long-established procedures of government, rather than a victorious Caesar who rode roughshod over them. But his thoughts were now more directed to the present company.

Was Scaurus still wealthy after supporting the loser in the civil war? Scaurus' father had been famous. He had married into the influential family of the Metelli, then at the height of their power. He had become Consul, Censor, Leader of the Senate. The man opposite Fufidius now might have made the consulship as well. Thirteen or fourteen years ago, as Aedile, he had built a temporary theatre for his gladiators that had people gasping at its sumptuous decoration. His villa on the Palatine Hill had seen society banquets of wild extravagance. But later, as Propraetor of Sardinia, he had so ruthlessly milked the inhabitants that he had been prosecuted for extortion. A six-strong defence counsel got him off, but the trial ruined his chances of the consulship.

Fufidius' head swam a little. Since Scaurus' father had been consul, more than sixty years had gone by. But the aura of greatness still clung to the man entertaining him.

"It's the end of the Republic," Scaurus was saying now. "Marius began it, opening up the army to all the landless ruffians in the country. I saw the levies for Caesar . . . more like beasts than men, a lot of them."

"The times are very difficult," agreed Fufidius. "I am told by Marcus Cicero that at Veii and Capena Caesar is having the land surveyed for allotments. It is very close to us here."

"I suppose Cicero is privy to the confidences of Caesar!"

"He has Caesar's ear, at least," returned Fufidius, trying to strike a lighter note. "They say all his latest *bons mots* are served up to Caesar along with his dinner."

Scaurus snorted. *"Bons mots!* It's no wonder Caesar's taking a course of emetics just now, so they say." He groaned and eased his position on the couch. "I could do with some *bons mots* to take my mind off things. Of course, you would know Cicero better than most, as you were his tribune in Cilicia."

Fufidius assented.

"I don't suppose you found your time there too onerous, did you? Not too much fighting took place in *his* governorship, by all accounts." Scaurus chuckled. He was drinking and talking himself into a good humour. "And if there had been any fighting, his brother would have done it for him."

Then, looking at Fufidius more keenly, he continued, "I heard that Cicero's accounts which he submitted after his administration didn't tally with his quaestor's, who had to make up the difference himself. It was a lot. Marcus Cicero talked about the *'elegantia'* of his administration. Well, he never had any trouble in clothing any of his operations with words—fine words—and I dare say his governorship of Cilicia was no exception. Perhaps his quaestor didn't think his administration so elegant!" Scaurus suddenly rounded on Fufidius and asked, "How did *you* do out of it, eh?"

Fufidius looked down to hide a smile and said quietly, "Tribunes and *contubernales* don't get a salary."

"Well, maintenance allowance and rewards for special service can sometimes be stretched a long way." Scaurus' eyes were knowledgeable as he surveyed the other.

"I managed to keep my head above water. Even well above," Fufidius admitted.

He was beginning to feel overwhelmed. To be reclining tête-à-tête with a patrician like Scaurus, while Scaurus gossiped in this intimate way! Slaves ran to and fro with fruit and cheese. One of them sponged down Marcus Scaurus' face from time to time.

"Your service overseas must have made you famous in your home town of Arpinum. I suppose your countrymen would have cast plenty of votes for you, had you wanted to pursue a political career in your home province."

Fufidius nodded. "If I had wanted . . . But I prefer to be a simple owner of farms and man of business. And to live in Rome."

"You're a quiet man, Fufidius. You keep your own counsel and you do well. Your estates speak for themselves."

Marcus Scaurus' eyes ran moodily over Fufidius. Fufidius— what an outlandish name! Could an Aemilius Scaurus be allied to a Fufidius? The obscure name from a poor mountain region. Names like Fundilii, Teredii, Terrasidii, Fufidii, they didn't hold much water at Rome. But Fufidius had wealth.

Outside the air seethed under the burning sun, and the earth baked. In the triclinium slaves waved wet fans and it was passably cool and dark. Marcus Scaurus was still talking and Fufidius was beginning to have to make an effort to follow him. He was not accustomed to drinking so much. Marcus Scaurus had talked of property again, especially of Fufidius' widespread holdings of land, and now he was talking of his son.

"He has seen her upon two occasions, I believe, and is delighted with her."

Fufidius jerked himself to attention. "He is?"

"Quite charmed. You must have been wondering why I wanted to talk . . ."

"To me?"

"Well, of course." Scaurus held the attention of Fufidius. "It is time my son settled down. I don't want him following his brother's example and getting into trouble by taking sides again against Caesar. The Greek and African campaigns were enough. I want him to marry and make a career befitting a Scaurus."

Fufidius shook himself mentally and tried to concentrate.

"I know he has been rather wild at times," Scaurus continued. "But he is still young. It would be a splendid match for your daughter."

Light dawned. Through fumes of wine, Fufidius tried to think.

Scaurus was offering marriage. The marriage of his young son to Fufa. Fufa, engaged to a patrician. Gnaeus Plancius, worthy son of a prosperous equestrian father, smiled on by Helvia and her brother Cinna as a suitable husband for Fufa, passed before Fufidius' hazy vision, then sailed off slowly like a respectable coaster, dependable but ordinary, while Lucius Scaurus raced into sight, a graceful and aristocratic yacht, eclipsing Plancius forever.

Of course Fufidius' wife Helvia should be consulted, and Gratidia too. Family conferences should be held, alternatives considered. But what alternative could hope to equal this dazzling prospect spread before him here and now? "Rather wild," Scaurus had said.

"He is still young." Scaurus was talking again. "In the flower of his age, your Cicero would say!"

"H'm. In the flower of his age!"

Scaurus' face had a reddish glow as he added, "Think it's a splendid thing myself. What do you say?"

Fufidius was two steps behind. Hesitate and the chance could be forever lost.

"Youth, yes of course, young men will be young men," he said hesitantly. Suddenly, good businessman and father as he was, he made his decision.

"Marcus Scaurus, you catch me by surprise," he declared candidly. "But I see the benefits of your suggestion. My daughter is thought to be beautiful and she has been carefully brought up. Our family is not on the illustrious level of yours, but we are well thought of."

Fufidius played for time. His head was spinning from emotion now as well as from wine. Concentration was difficult.

"Of course, there's the dowry to be settled," Scaurus said clearly and deliberately. "My son's career is going to be an expensive business. But we are two good men, and between two good men there can be only trust, don't you agree? I think we shall meet no insurmountable difficulties in the matter of the dowry."

"Ah yes, the dowry." The splendid vision gained solidity now. Fufidius' mind always embraced figures with ease. He prepared to bargain.

Scaurus named a figure and Fufidius began to point to the adequacy of a lower figure. Scaurus cut in.

"I have never had a daughter," he said. "Our women have always come to us with *manus* . . ." he paused, "and so assumed the status of a noble whatever the level of their family."

Fufidius waited.

"With *manus* your daughter will share fully in our lives," Scaurus went on. "What Lucius may achieve will be her achievement as well. It is more suitable, do you not think? And what comes to Lucius, of course, comes to her as well."

"And what property she brings will belong to your family absolutely," Fufidius observed.

Scaurus laughed easily. "Surely *formalities* need be no obstacle to all this!" and he looked at Fufidius questioningly.

After a time Fufidius nodded. His mind was busy with property valuations. When it came to the hard realities, the two men understood that the sum named by Scaurus would be reduced to some extent.

Marcus Scaurus was relieved that the decision was made. Not that there could ever have been any doubt of the acceptance of his suggestion. This marriage would lift the Fufidii daughter to a social level which she could never have expected and her whole family would benefit. Fufidius, however, could scarcely have known how desperately in debt the Scauri were or that young Lucius' reputation was already such that not all families of his own rank would receive him.

Scaurus raised his glass. "We are in agreement, Quintus Fufidius. So let us drink to our good work."

"You have been in the company of a young man and without my permission, Fufidia," said her father next morning.

Fufidia, this fair child of a dark father, looked distantly at him from her own world. Then ducked her head to conceal a smile.

"Tell me the circumstances, Fufidia," he went on, as sternly as he could.

She looked up then, her eyes not quite on his and with as absent an expression as he had ever seen on her face. "Nothing, Papa. Only, we went to see the dancing."

"H'm. Well, I am told by his father that the young man wants to marry you."

She looked vaguer than ever, but her eyes gleamed. "Yes, Papa."

"What do you feel about it?"

"I want to."

And Fufidia retreated wholly into her other world again—a world of perfect love, where Callirrhoe-Fufidia was united with Chaereas-Lucius and they never stopped kissing. What her father told her was no surprise to her. She had never supposed that anything but marriage could ensue with this youth of, by now, heroic proportions and godlike beauty.

"I will tell your mother as soon as she gets back," her father said.

He was just a little uneasy, remembering the extravagant love of Helvia for her daughter. But there—it was too wonderful a marriage opportunity to be imperilled by delays.

IV

From Tusculum, in a gorgeous dawn, his carriage wound down
the slopes of those volcanic mountains, through woods of ilex
and chestnut and elm, through the *vineta* of their lower reaches,
down to Lake Albanus, then to Aricia, where he owned land—
land with rich dark soil that bore vines and fruit trees and the
famous strawberries. This property overlooked the intense, mysterious green of the smaller lake, whose perfect circle was called
the mirror of Diana, reflecting the sacred wood near the temple
of the goddess.

Fufidius had business at the temple. He might laugh at Gratidia and her offerings, but all the same he carried with him a
terra-cotta votive of a gouty foot—this to thank Diana for what
relief she had already afforded Gratidia. A gift of money passed
to a priestess and prayers were offered. Fufidius made his way
down the steep temple steps, out to the great terrace of ruddy
travertine. As he gazed down at the gleaming mirror of Diana,
the sky seemed to darken and a gust of wind to rush by—or else
the goddess sighed. For a moment, all the sounds of that morning, the voices of the peasants on the land and the bird song and
rustle of trees ceased. Fufidius shivered and involuntarily looked
back at the huge retaining walls against the mountainside, and
stood unable to walk down from the high terrace. Then just as
suddenly everyday life resumed about him, the sun was hot on
his back, the country smells strong. He breathed again that special atmosphere of the place—a curious blend of agricultural labour and lazy holiday calm imposed by the luxury villas nestling
on these hills, one of which belonged to Caesar himself, together
with all the bustling traffic in religion around the temple.

He reflected, as he was carried up to Aricia, that some of the
earthenware votive offerings were made in Arretium by Helvia's
relatives. If only indirectly, Diana was of practical use to the

Fufidii. And the Fufidii to Diana! This was a comforting thought
to him, unsettled still by that premonition, fleeting as it was, of
divine anger.

Next morning, on the sixteen-mile journey to Rome by the Via
Appia, his thoughts were on the marriage contract. Agreed on in
a rose haze of wine, it gave him—cold sober as he was now—
nothing but satisfaction. It would cost him money, that was all.
Marcus Scaurus, patrician, of great wealth only a few years ago
when—Fufidius' eyes grew troubled—Eucharis had played as a
mime in his house . . . And the image of this Greek slave girl,
who had crept from the fringes of his existence to a hardly dis-
pensable role to him, stirred now, displacing thoughts of the
marriage contract for two whole miles of the Via Appia.

He had got her with child one balmy summer night just before he left Arpinum for Cilicia. She had borne that child in his
absence, in defiance of Helvia, and had later run away.

Now he thought of his secret search for her in Rome on his
return a year later. He had sought out Parthenios, the Greek
grammarian and poet. It had been Cinna—Helvia's brother—
who had brought Parthenios back with him from Bithynia years
ago—and Eucharis too. Greek booty. Parthenios was by now a
notable literary figure in his own right.

"You surely know," Parthenios had said, in his soft voice,
having bowed Fufidius into his inner sanctum in a way that infu-
riated Fufidius. "You surely know Eucharis has done very well.
She is now a very clever mime. She is with the company of
Publius Syrus."

There followed a night so little in character for him that
Fufidius would always blush to remember it. He had slunk up
the Palatine Hill and watched through the trees, from as near as
he could, the moving, lovely floods of light from a thousand
torches and lanterns, and listened to the music, heard the laughter, from the palatial villa of the Aemilii Scauri. Somewhere, in
there, Eucharis performed her mime—and worse, perhaps.

"I'd not worry about her; she could be the toast of Rome?"
Respectfully, Parthenios had mocked him.

Grimly, Fufidius had stood in the shadows and pictured—his
imagination spurred to extremes of explicit lewdness—the orgies

of fashionable aristocrats that might follow a mimed performance. He saw the lounging figures in their rich robes, the silver goblets and gold plate, the frescoed hall, the rich marbles, smelt the perfumes, watched Eucharis dance for them, hardly moving, but with a suggestion in each slight movement.

And he had ground his teeth, suffering pangs—for the first time in his life—of love and jealousy. For a slave! Fine behaviour for a Roman knight, father of a respected family, descendant of a many-branched family tree, which counted amongst its far reaches links with notable Italian families. Fufidius, worth five million *sestertii* in lands and investments, stepson of Marcus Caesius, *maxime et familiaris et necessarius* of Cicero . . .

The next day he had found Eucharis in her small apartment in the Subura. She had dropped at his feet, as though to evade his fury. He had pulled her up and at the mere touch of those small, firm hands, all the long-denied love of her had come flooding back. She was wearing the diaphanous robe of the actress and through it her body was all the more inviting. She told him of her despair when Helvia had ordered her to abort and made it clear she had been in fear for her life. Fufidius was puzzled. It must, he concluded, be because Helvia suspected the child was his, and that the girl might use this as a lever in all sorts of ways. He did not mention that he might have told her to do the same, had he been there.

"The *domina* wanted me to kill my child."

"Yet you did keep the child and she found you work as a wet nurse," he demurred.

"*Nutrix!*" The scorn was strong in her voice.

The wife of Titus Fadius, to whom Helvia had sent Eucharis, had been a bad mistress. Eucharis had milk only for one baby and little over. She had finally run away, taking the boy.

"Parthenios was afraid to interfere, saying a runaway slave had no chance if caught. But he helped me all the same and I got this job as a *mima.*"

"And you think it better than to be a *nutrix?*" demanded Fufidius. "To expose your body for the pleasure of old lechers!"

She covered her face. "It was to find money to care for my child—who is your child," she whispered.

"What's this?" Rummaging in her little chest, he had drawn out a gold necklace and a set of gold thigh bands. Trappings of the *meretrix*.

"They were given me, because I danced well. It was all in order. The wives sat round as well. I danced against a beautiful fresco. It was very artistic."

"Artistic! I'm sure."

Several months later, after long consideration, he had decided to free her. He had taken her up before the Praetor Urbanus and by the ancient act of *manumissio vindictar* she had become a Roman citizen. He still remembered the way her face had shone at the Praetor's formal words, *"Eam liberam addico.* I pronounce her to be free."

Fufidius had then paid the five percent of her purchased value which he owed to the state on the transaction. Henceforth Eucharis would bear his name—Fufidia Quinti liberta Eucharis.

The only drawback for her was that her little boy remained a slave.

Time had passed. Now, five years after, Fufidius could be well pleased. Once more he had made a good bargain. With his agreement and his capital, but on her suggestion, she had begun a little publishing business on her premises. Beginning with two slaves, she now had a set of eight scribes and could produce twenty-five books a month. They were books of a notable fineness, on the best papyrus rolls, tastefully written and charmingly decorated with a design of leaves and rosettes, intricately entwined, which she had herself created. So while at fifteen she had attracted him, at twenty-one enchanted him, now at twenty-nine her business acumen, her underlying toughness had shown her a person worthy of his respect as well. Besides, her physical charms had only increased with the years and he seldom felt the need to have other women.

Fufidius gave a curt order now to the driver to increase the horses' pace and he tightened his grip on his sword. This part of the Via Appia was less crowded, even lonely. He could remember it lined with the crucified corpses of slaves—six thousand of them—the wooden crosses creaking in the wind under their grim burden. The slave revolt had struck terror throughout the country.

But he didn't want to think of such things now. What he
wanted now was Eucharis, with her pretty little feet on his shoulders.

Fufidius reached Eucharis' house late in the day. She greeted
him with delight. She was even daintier, he thought, and more
pliant than ever. Her lovely body twisted and clung as he pulled
her to him. He undressed her at once, rapturous as always to feel
those smooth arms around him, those supple thighs moving. He
groaned with delight.

Outside in the corridor, two women servants clasped hands.

"How they enjoy themselves," said one, her ear to the door.

"It is always like that," replied the other.

At a small scream from within they sighed enviously.

"I must go now."

They had lain together an hour or more.

"Not so soon."

She knelt at his feet and looked up lovingly. "Your voice is
like a bell in your chest—a great deep bell."

He laughed delightedly.

"Marite," she breathed.

"Mulier," he replied, a shade less enthusiastically.

It was a joke between them for her to call him "husband" and
for him to reply "wife." She knew it could never be.

"I want you to see Pamphilus when he returns from school."

Their son had the cleverness of the Greek—handsome as well,
now eight years old.

"And there are some things I wanted to talk about."

"No business just now."

"You said we might buy ten new scribes. You remember you
agreed it was time to feed the profits back into the business. We
have more work than we can handle now."

"Not yet. Not now."

"I don't displease you?"

"Of course not." He rubbed his face against hers.

"Domine?"

"Yes?"

"Our boy grows fast."

He was silent, suddenly withdrawn, sensing trouble.

"Think, *Domine,* our little boy is to grow up a slave. Your child. He resembles you, as well." It was not in the least true, but she insisted so charmingly.

"Not really," he mumbled.

"A lot."

"I have not been ungenerous, Eucharis."

"And I have worked very hard." She looked intently at him. Suddenly she said, *"Domine!* Adopt him! Adopt him into your family. Free him now so that the adoption may take place. Let him grow up as your son. As a Roman citizen, his life is secure. As your son, he will find preferment."

He shook his head. "Eucharis, it is not possible. Now less than ever."

She was trembling. With an effort she kept control of herself. "Then, will you give me the advance of the one thousand *sestertii* you promised?"

"What was that?"

"You promised me this before you left for Gaul."

"I don't remember," he said uncertainly.

She was lying again. But it was nearly always in small things. She confused others elegantly and prettily. He could only admire her.

"You must not ask for so much just now."

"I need this money very much."

"I have no ready cash at the moment. Don't forget young Quintus has been eating up money in Athens. He is due back in Rome any day now and will need even more until he gets established as an advocate. You know most of my money is tied up. And I have a new commitment—a big commitment—due very soon. In fact, I will have to reduce your monthly payments by about a quarter for some time."

"No!"

"Fufidia is to marry," he said. "She is to marry a young man of rank. I will need every penny I have for the dowry."

"May I know whom she is to marry?"

"Lucius Scaurus. The younger son of Marcus Aemilius Scaurus." He could not keep the satisfaction from his voice.

"Not Lucius Scaurus!" In surprise he saw her positively recoil at the name.

"Why *not* Scaurus?"

She brushed his question aside. Her voice rose now. "You are not prepared to do anything for our son, but for the daughter of *Helvia—everything!*" Her eyes blazed.

"An odd way to refer to my daughter, to say nothing of my wife. Stop this, Eucharis!"

"My boy's future is nothing to you!"

"Eucharis! Don't shout." His own voice was rising. "You know I have never begrudged the boy anything."

"You have given him money. That's all!"

His head reeled. Never had she shouted at him. The adoption —did she mean it seriously? She must know that Helvia would never agree. Helvia would fear for her own children's inheritance. Once adopted, Pamphilus could legally inherit from Fufidius. Eucharis could surely not compare her own child with Fufidia or young Quintus. A boy born in slavery—even now, only the son of a freedwoman.

Fufidius prepared to depart. Before he left he gave Eucharis a brooch and some money, more than he had intended.

Left to herself, Eucharis trembled, cried, regained control and finally went to her son Pamphilus, as soon as he got back from school. That bright little boy raised his keen eyes to hers. He was so much her own quick-witted son. She told him little, but he knew all about his mother's affairs. She thought he knew everything.

"Has my father been here, Mamma?" For he spoke of Fufidius always as his father.

Eucharis sighed and nodded.

"I think Fufidius will adopt me in the end," said the child. "I make myself charming whenever he is here, and—Roman. I model myself on Fufidius for him to see." Pamphilus threw back his head and stumped up and down, stern and dignified. "I am not ungenerous, my dear," he mimed. "How much do you want? Just name a figure . . . five hundred *sestertii?* The thing is done! I just don't have it on me at the moment, but once the Campanian rents are in, you'll have it," Pamphilus curled his fingers and gestured, his hand close to his face, "at twenty-five percent!"

"Pamphilus!" Eucharis looked almost fearfully at him. He was almost too advanced for his years. "I would not be sure of being adopted or of anything just now. And I beg you to keep quiet about it. At school and at home."

"I do not chatter, Mamma."

"Get on with your homework now."

She picked up a tablet on which he had been practising his writing. Twenty times he had copied out in his neat hand:

S.P.Q.R.
SENATUS POPULUSQUE ROMANUS
S.P.Q.R
SENATUS POPULUSQUE ROMANUS. Senate and people of Rome.

But halfway down the tablet it had changed to:

S.P.Q.R.
SUNT PORCI QUEI ROMANI. They are pigs, these Romans!

"Oh, Pamphilus!" She paled and snatched the tablet, obliterating the pun.

"Never, never do such a thing, Pamphilus! A Greek is a most convenient scapegoat in Rome. Oh, be careful! Always be careful!"

V

After leaving Eucharis, Fufidius hurried home as fast as his litter-bearers could carry him, eager now to give Helvia his news. But that brother of hers was there. No mistaking the eight bearers waiting outside—Cinna's Bithynians, the colour of amber, strong enough to bear a ton of marble on their muscular shoulders. They went everywhere with him and had done so since he had acquired them—along with Parthenios and Eucharis—in Bithynia in 65. Showy, thought Fufidius. He was good about lending them out to his friends, though. They made an excellent bodyguard as well. Cinna was a tall slight man in build. No weakling, thought Fufidius, but his real strength was all in his tongue. And in his eyes, he added. Piercing blue eyes that disconcerted by their intensity and seemed to see through you and far beyond the matter in hand.

They were in the garden, Helvia sitting on the stone edge of the fountain, Cinna lounging against it looking at her. Helvia's lips were parted as though an important question hung in the air and she was considering her answer. Such was the atmosphere of inner accord that Fufidius felt himself an intruder. At the sound of his feet on the pebbles as he crossed the courtyard, skirting the potted shrubs, Cinna swung round, his thin tanned face wearing an absent look. But then Helvia slid down from the fountain and the courtyard was suddenly loud with greetings.

"Quintus! *Bene redis!* Safe returned, thanks to the gods!"

"Oh, Quintus! Our son is on his way back from Athens. We've just had news."

"Excellent!" Fufidius was excited at this. Young Quintus had been gone two years.

Helvia's face was tinted by the southern sun and her eyes sparkled now. Fufidius, reinstated as master of the house after that flickering instant of exclusion, was finding it good to be home and to have them hang on his words, especially Helvia. What a good wife she was to him. Not only virtuous but rich. The dowry she had brought him had been considerable. Valuable property in the Po valley, the rents from which had built the villa in Tusculum. She had also brought him almost one million *sestertii*, her share in the proceeds of the pottery business her father had owned in Arretium. Her father had died soon after her marriage, and his estate had been divided between Cinna, who was unmarried and childless, and Helvia. Unless Cinna married, it was probable that all the wealth of the Helvii would finally come to Helvia's children by Fufidius.

"Wait till you see the household linen and clothing I got in Narbo. You feel at home up there, as it's got a real Roman stamp to it. Built on the square. We went up by the Via Aurelia, to avoid the head winds by ship . . ."

Elated now, Fufidius relived his journey as he told them.

Cinna rose eventually. "I must go. I couldn't before, as there is an infernal bore on my track."

"Those Bithynian bearers of yours will always give you away! I hope you leave them at home when you visit the ladies!" Fufidius joked.

"You wouldn't have me deprive a lady, would you? Anyway, they're half the reason for my popularity with them. They simply love my bearers and are always borrowing them." Cinna's eyes danced now, boring into Fufidius.

Helvia rose abruptly, upsetting a glass of wine. Fufidius saw her give her brother a venomous look. He changed the subject hastily. Helvia was so straitlaced. Unfairly, she now abused a servant who was not wiping up the mess quickly enough. Women were so changeable.

"I have to call on old Valerius Cato," announced her brother. "He's not well. How I envy you, Quintus, free to come and go. I shall be confined to the city all next year."

"But why?"

"From the tenth of December next I shall be a Tribune of the *plebs.*"

"I don't want you to be Tribune!" Helvia burst out. "You'll forever be at the mercy of people wanting you to submit things to Caesar and your doors will never be locked."

"I won't get down south again for a while," he agreed.

"You as well . . ." Fufidius understood suddenly that Cinna had been in Pompeii with Helvia.

Helvia rushed on. "I have a presentiment. It'll end badly. Holding office under a dictator . . ."

"Ah, but that dictator is Caesar," Cinna said slowly.

"Is that meant to console me?"

"As he is Fortune's favourite, yes, of course," her brother returned lightly, as he rose and went out to rouse up his sleeping bearers.

Alone with Helvia at last, Fufidius said, "Should we be glad or sorry for him? Why does he want to be Tribune? To propose motions and veto motions, as the handmaiden of Caesar!"

Helvia shrugged, suddenly dispirited. "You saw Fufidia?"

"Yes. You shouldn't have left her, Helvia."

"What's wrong?" she said sharply.

"Nothing." He paced the terrace, looking at her from time to time. "Oh, nothing. Nothing at all."

She could tell he was bursting with news.

"What have you to tell me?" she asked, going pale.

"Quite a lot." He paused. "I have arranged a marriage for her."

Helvia jerked violently. "What!"

"A good marriage. One that will certainly please you. She'll be married into a famous house."

Rigid now, her eyes brilliant, Helvia said no word.

"A patrician family, my dear. Old stock. Our neighbours in Tusculum."

"Patricians!" Helvia was caught completely by surprise. Her blood raced. "Who?"

"It is the younger son of Marcus Aemilius Scaurus."

"You arranged this in *Gaul?*"

"In Tusculum. I was invited to dine with the father. He proposed it then. The young man has seen our daughter and admires her."

"Over dinner you arranged the marriage of my daughter! Over dinner! Without consulting me! Oh no! And what . . . what does Fufidia think of it?"

"She couldn't be more pleased."

Helvia's hands frantically pleated and unpleated a fold of her robe. "Scaurus!" Her brain worked feverishly. "Isn't there a Scaurus with Sextus Pompeius in Spain? The family opposes Caesar."

"Not now."

"What *are* they now?"

"Who knows from one day to the next what he is?" demanded Fufidius. "They're still the oldest patrician stock."

Despite herself, Helvia's eyes gleamed now. She might be furious at his arranging this behind her back, but he knew her respect for rank. "What about money?" she asked abruptly.

"Well, of course, you don't marry into such a family for nothing. The details have to be discussed. Scaurus first suggested two million *sestertii.*"

"Oh, Quintus! What have you done? It is a fortune!"

"We can afford it, I think," he said heavily.

"Are the Scauri worth two million *sestertii?*" she returned.

Fufidius was stung to anger.

"Let me tell you one more thing, woman! When I got up to Tusculum, there wasn't a soul around. Gratidia was asleep, Fufidia nowhere in sight. Scaurus told me that during your absence—*your* absence let me say—Fufidiola spent a good deal of time with young Scaurus on the day of the Vinalia . . ."

"Through the drunkenness of *your* relative, no doubt!"

He shrugged. "Anything could have happened. Surely it's better they marry!"

Helvia rounded on him. "If you really think that, you should have killed the young man. Any self-respecting father would!" Her voice fell and she practically hissed. "But you . . . oh no, Fufidius simply makes a marriage contract. Fufidius cares nothing for our reputation."

"Stop it! I tell you I don't know what happened! Now just you look at this." He rummaged in his box and threw a scroll at her. "I found this. This is the kind of thing your daughter reads on the sly. Chariton, of Aphrodisias." He slammed down another scroll. *"The Woman from Samos.* Menander." Another. "Parthenios. *Erotic Tales . . ."*

He watched beads of sweat form on her forehead.

"Now calm down, Helvia. I have done my best for Fufidia."
He waited for her to say, "In a drunken orgy."

In answer to an urgent note from his sister, Cinna was early at
the house again next morning. Helvia was no longer angry but
consumed with excited wonder.

"Gaius! He's arranged to marry Fufidia off to Lucius Scaurus!"

"A Scaurus!" Cinna was startled. "A Scaurus," he repeated
slowly.

"Quintus says Fufidia wants to," Helvia rushed on eagerly.
"They've seen each other, she and the boy. I have too. He *is*
handsome and was charming to me, simply charming. And all
the time you and I were thinking of—"

"Yes, young Plancius. But this is better. Let me think. Lucius
Scaurus. I don't know him but I've seen him. He's attractive.
Fufa wouldn't be the only girl who has fallen for him." He
paused and went on more slowly. "It's well known the father is
up to his ears in debt. His Palatine villa was sold years ago. That
son of his in Spain must have eaten up much of what remained of
his money."

Cinna left soon after, his manner preoccupied. He promised
to visit Helvia at Tusculum later in the summer.

VI

In the following weeks, Fufidius' household revolved about arrangements for the wedding to come. A date had been set in late February, when the Feast of the Dead was safely over. March or April would have been better, but Lucius Scaurus would leave for the eastern campaign in March. Negotiations for the dowry had been complicated and prolonged. A figure was finally set at 1.5 million *sestertii.* What form it should take—an all-important matter—was still under discussion. Rich Fufidius might be, but so many of his assets were in the form of property or other immovables. Ready cash was always short. Fufidius would return from the interviews with Scaurus worried and short-tempered.

Helvia paled when she heard the final sum.

"I am to pay rather more than the usual third on the first installment," her husband admitted. "Scaurus wants all he can get. Lucius has to establish his own household and then there are the expenses of outfitting him for the Parthian war. I shall have to call on your property, Helvia, if I am not to realise on the Campanian land."

She stiffened and Fufidius added, "You know I have large sums out at interest that I don't want to call in. You know about Caesar's law on debt. I've lost heavily on all that unproductive land I've been forced to take over from debtors in the Ager Laurens at pre-war prices."

"I paid for Tusculum," Helvia reminded him.

"Yes. And it doesn't give much return either, except for wine and a little olive oil. The villa is a luxury."

"Oh, Quintus, all that money from Cilicia is yours. And what of your eight large properties and smaller tenant-farms as well, to say nothing of your Rome apartments. *And* your team of gladiators!"

"There is no end to my commitments nowadays. Don't forget

our son has eaten up a good deal in Athens and now there are his expenses here."

"As well as your ex-slave-woman's needs of course."

"As well as the comparatively slight expenditure on the little publishing business which is proving such a success," he retorted. "Helvia, I need money from you, quite apart from your dowry."

She thought for a while.

"Would Fufidia's dowry be returned in the case of death?"

"Whose death?"

"Why, Lucius'. *He* is the one who goes off to fight, isn't he?"

"Oh, if Lucius should die," Fufidius said, his eyes shifting rapidly from Helvia and back again, his mouth tightening, "I could reclaim it. I must draw up an agreement about that before the marriage."

"What if Fufidia wants a divorce?" asked Helvia sharply.

"Divorce? Well, of course," he said rapidly, "she would first have to be . . . what's the word? Remancipated."

"Remancipated?"

"She will be in the power of Lucius. Like a daughter to him."

There was a tense silence. Helvia's eyes burned into him. Then she said, ominously, "Quintus, have you agreed to a *manus* marriage, so that she'll no longer have any claim to her dowry or her inheritance from you?"

Fufidius shrugged and perambulated. "Scaurus wanted it," he muttered.

Helvia fought with herself to speak calmly. *"No* woman is married *cum manu* now."

"It's not true." He shook his head.

"Why?" she burst out. "Why, why did you have to agree? She won't have a thing she can call her own! How—*Mehercle!*—how can you surrender your little Fufidia to those bloodsuckers!"

"Helvia! I can't bear any more! I have already agreed. Now will you please answer me? Will you contribute to the dowry?"

She gave a cry, high and despairing, and springing up turned her back. "The dowry! Oh, the dowry!" She swung back towards him, fighting for control. "I must consider it. I must consider it."

He knew that meant she wanted to consult with her brother.

He shuffled uneasily. Then he remembered, "I have something else to say to you."

She quietened, staring at him.

"I want to know," he said deliberately, "if there is any significance in an object I have seen in your apartment."

"What object?"

"A little oil lamp. And part of it is a figure—the figure of Isis. It's the sort of cheap trash you pick up in shrines."

She said no word.

"Am I to understand you have some interest there? I know your aunt in Pompeii is an initiate, more's the pity."

"You've searched my possessions," she countered.

"Are you an initiate?"

She shook her head.

"Helvia, do you go to meetings?"

She shifted restlessly and protested, "If my aunt does, you have nothing to say. If I—"

"This is not Pompeii," he returned. "Who worships Isis here in Rome? Freed slaves and aliens! The meetings have been banned countless times."

She said in a low voice, "Caesar has lifted the ban on worship."

"By order of that paramour of his, I suppose!"

"Cleopatra is a worshipper, of course," she admitted.

"What I cannot understand," he exploded, "is why you're attracted to this sort of thing when everyone who matters holds it in contempt! Just when we've made this alliance with a noble house, you have to mix with people who worship dogs and snakes and cats and bulls and monkeys!"

Helvia, motionless, bent her head, and his rage poured over her.

"Nothing I have done could have given me more comfort," she answered quietly. "And comfort I need."

"Helvia! You know I've always left family religion to you, as is right and proper. Do our household gods mean nothing now?"

She turned a tragic face on him for an instant and shook her hands helplessly. But she would say nothing more.

He left with a warning: "I absolutely forbid you to attend meetings. Heaven knows what repercussions there could be for all of us if it were to become known. And with this marriage coming up! And what's more," he caught her roughly by the shoulder, "I don't want to hear another word from you against the Scauri!"

As soon as she left Fufidius, Helvia hurried to Gratidia's room, where the old woman sat being read to by a slave. At the sight of Helvia's face, she sent the man off.

Helvia burst out immediately, "He has made a marriage *in manu* for Fufidia!" She had no need to specify who had made it.

Gratidia said nothing. She sat motionless, her eyes searching Helvia's.

"She is to be completely in the power of that family. Lost to us, with nothing of her own for the rest of her life!"

Gratidia contented herself with saying, "There are fewer such marriages these days."

"Oh, can you wonder at it!"

"There's one thing that's good. She joins the Scaurus family, but she will inherit on the death of the father just like a daughter."

Helvia cut in rudely, "What a prize—to inherit from that penniless old brute, after he has got through all her money!"

"Come, there are laws about dowry, laws to protect her."

"And she cannot divorce him!" Helvia stormed on heedlessly.

"I know of a woman married *in manu* who got her father to arrange a divorce for her."

Helvia wasn't listening. She wrung her hands. "Lost to me! I can do nothing for her. Give her nothing, without it being swallowed up by that exhausted old rake and his son, so he can dance at fashionable dinner parties. I can see now that this is what comes of marrying a daughter to . . . to a name without money."

"Calm down, do!"

"The dowry!" Helvia was practically shouting now. "Do you know how much it'll be, very probably? One and a half million

sestertii! Oh . . . just a beginning, that. A great part of it immediately, to be made straight over to their creditors. Then, I am to
hand over farmland and who know what else for them to sell as
soon as they can get their hands on it!''

She ran from the room in a rage.

VII

Cinna was kept busy with his tribunate approaching. He had also to visit properties outside Rome. On his return, however, he sent for two young poets of his acquaintance who cultivated the high society of the time. In his little house near the Forum he pressed good wine on them, confident always of the truth of the dictum *in vino veritas*. He found the two young men well informed on the life-style of Lucius Scaurus.

"He loves the life here," declared the first. "The most determined battle he'll ever fight will be to delay his return to the camp. He so enjoys what is on offer in Rome. We see him often at receptions. Appears to gamble a lot and is said to owe money."

"Elegant, insolent and easy," put in the other.

"Easy? What do you mean?" asked Cinna.

"If your tastes run in a certain direction and you've got plenty of money to entertain in style, with gifts for special guests, then Lucius finds it easy to accept your invitations."

They gossiped at length about Lucius Scaurus and several other young men no longer welcomed by some of the more old-fashioned good families. Cinna was a worried man by the time the other two left.

A chance meeting the next day with the old senator Considius did not lessen his worry. It took place in the barber's shop and Cinna, waiting until the barber had finished plucking the senator's bushy eyebrows, had only to mention Lucius' name.

"Lucius Scaurus? He served under Scipio in the African war against Caesar. After the battle at Thapsus he turned up somehow in Rome and he's been here now for a year or so. It's thought that his mother fixed it."

The barber finished Considius off by slapping a perfumed lotion over his face and the old man moved to a bench near Cinna.

"His mother Mucia—a much married lady," Considius smiled, "of notorious infidelity. She left Lucius' father for Pompeius and *he* divorced her for her goings on with Caesar. But she's still a favourite of Caesar and there's no doubt that a word in his ear had young Lucius pardoned. Now Lucius is a regular young man about town."

"In the Greek campaign wasn't he? And I'm told he was in command of a troop of horse. On that record, he should go far, I imagine," probed Cinna.

Considius' newly shaven old face had creased into a thousand wrinkles of merriment.

"Lucius Scaurus? Not according to the story I had from my son. We have a business in Utica, and after the fighting was over, my son was trapped in his own warehouse by a mob while the looting was going on. Might have been cut to pieces, but an old soldier went in with his sword and stopped the drunken idiots. Single-handed. Ninnius was the soldier's name. My son got him a passage back to Italy afterwards and now I've got him managing one of my farms near here. Capable man. Now if you want to know about Lucius Scaurus, you should talk to Ninnius. He was with Scaurus just before the battle at Thapsus."

Gladly, Cinna accepted the suggestion that Considius should have Ninnius come to Rome to talk to him. Only three nights later Cinna sat with the senator in his house waiting for Ninnius to arrive.

"He's an old soldier," Considius told Cinna. "You know the type—coarse, fearless, capable of great endurance, sell his sister for a coin or rape yours if he got the chance. Absolutely truthful, below his dignity to lie. You can depend on what he says. He feels indebted to me for my helping in setting him up here. He even married a lively young wife recently who'll give him a son soon. Don't be put off by his crudeness."

The man who entered just then was powerfully built, of some forty years, with a sun-darkened face and hair already streaked with grey. His voice was a deep rumble. He rested strong hands on the table as he began his story. He was nothing loath to talk.

"Thapsus? Thapsus town lies on a narrow tongue of land between the sea and the lagoon, so both the armies were in sight of each other. Our general Scipio was afraid that Caesar might have reinforcements up north, out of sight. You see, Caesar is clever beyond belief. And not only in fighting. In talking, too. All the time he was sending word that if we changed sides we'd get land, booty, anything you like." His lips curled ironically. "Our general Scipio promised us a free Senate!"

"Yes, yes, but about Lucius Scaurus . . ." Cinna urged him, well aware of Caesar's hold over the common people.

"Lucius Scaurus was in charge of another man and me on a mission just before the battle. We was to go up the coast and make a long sweep beyond the marsh of Moknine to reconnoitre for any sign of reinforcements. We left at dawn, going north, riding over country that'd make you weep if you was a farmer— wheat unharvested and rotting every which way you looked."

The man's eyes gazed far into the distance and Cinna feared they would have to put up with a typical rambling account of campaigns past and already half forgotten. But Ninnius got to the point quickly now.

"The other man was a young 'un, from way up in Narbonese Gaul. Couldn't take his eyes off Lucius Scaurus and Scaurus didn't mind. I thought something might develop. Well, we rode most of the day. Scaurus kept us going farther and farther up the coast instead of circling inland. Said it was to look for food and fodder. The weather got very bad and we were lucky to find shelter in some abandoned farm buildings and luckier still to find stores of wine and food hidden there. We would have risked the horses' legs if we'd gone on, so we got ourselves cosy for the night."

The old soldier paused and then grinned broadly.

"We found plenty of wine, so we all got drunk. Right pissed, you might say. We swapped stories—war stories. I told them enough of the blood and guts I'd seen in my twenty years. Once I had Lucius about to cry when I talked about good-looking young men of his own age with their faces split open by Roman swords. He was a pretty young officer, this Lucius Scaurus, sexy as a girl. I could see that he and the Gaul were getting excited as we went on drinking. I went off to sleep, but they made enough noise to wake me. Couldn't see much, but the Gaul was on top, enjoying himself. I was half minded to have a poke myself. But I'd sooner wait for what a woman's got."

"You mean that Scaurus is a *cinaedus?*" demanded Cinna peremptorily.

"He certainly is, sir," the man replied. "They had another go during the night, taking it in turns. But that's only part of the story."

"You're sure of what you're telling us?" Considius asked sharply.

"I don't lie, sir. You know me better than that," the old soldier said simply.

"Go on."

"Next morning, Lucius Scaurus was still so drunk that he couldn't stand. We put him on his horse but he just fell off. Twice. You'd have choked yourself laughing to see an officer of the general's staff not able to sit on his horse! He just managed to tell us to leave him and his horse and go back to Thapsus. He would come as soon as he could, he said.

"Well, he was still our officer, so we did as we were told. But I wasn't really convinced. After a mile or so, we stopped to look back. You can see a long way in that cursed brown country. We saw a horse being loaded and a rider jump up with no problem and then head away from us. I tell you—I would have killed him myself, officer or no officer. To desert just before a battle! A soldier doesn't do that."

Ninnius shook his head.

"I tried, but I couldn't catch up with him. His horse was faster. So the Gaul and I, we returned to our army, and when we got there, the battle had already begun. By that night there were ten thousand dead, so they say. The young Gaul was one. He died fighting. But there was no Lucius Scaurus on the battlefield. I heard later that he had turned up after the battle safe and sound in Utica and used his influence to get back to Rome quickly. Of course, he was related to the General. He'll have a good story and you tell me that Caesar has pardoned him. Who's to believe a simple soldier like me? So it's no business of mine, but I spit on Lucius Scaurus."

Cinna had a long and troubled ride to Tusculum to tell Helvia what he had learned.

VIII

Helvia was in the garden of the villa on hands and knees, grop-
ing in the waters of the little canal where multi-coloured fish
darted.

"I've dropped my bracelet in." She groped, then raised a
moist and flushed face, holding up the wet ornament. Her fair
hair was tumbled. She had the sort of look about her that she had
as a child. Cinna was to think later it was the last time he saw her
happy, in those days of calm before the ravaging storm.

Helvia scrambled to her feet and shook out a dripping fold of
her gown. *"Da mi basium!"* She raised her face.

He embraced her, then pushed her gently away. "Fufidia?" he
enquired.

"Fufa is in raptures. It's nothing but Lucius Scaurus, and nothing but good. She thinks only of him. Indeed, he is exceptionally
good-looking! He looks just as a noble should. His features are
so refined, so delicate!"

"Delicate, yes. Oh yes."

Her face froze at her brother's expression. "What do you
mean?"

"I know a senator called Quintus Considius," Cinna said
abruptly.

"Ah . . ." Helvia sat down on a wooden bench, still holding
him with her eyes.

The massed roses put out their heavy scent in the hot air. From
the pergola above their heads a rose hip bounced down suddenly
and then there was only the sound of the little fountain dribbling
into the pool in the middle of the sun-drenched courtyard.

"He's an elderly man, now, this Considius," continued Cinna.
"And a good man. You can trust what he says. I talked to him
because of what he knew of Lucius Scaurus in the African campaign." Cinna paced up and down several times and then said,

"It seems that Lucius is hardly noted for his old-fashioned virtue."

He stopped and the sunlight, dancing on his face through the quivering foliage above, mocked his words.

"Just what do you mean?"

"While they were on reconnaissance just before the battle near Thapsus, Lucius Scaurus and two other men found a cache of wine on an abandoned farm. They got drunk and after quite a night of it Lucius insisted he was too sick to move. The other two went back to Thapsus. Lucius never saw the battle at all, but turned up safe and sound when it was all over."

"He deserted?"

"That would be a fair interpretation. But I'm afraid there is more," her brother said carefully. "I've listened to a detailed account from one of those two soldiers of how Lucius and the other young man went together several times during the night. With Scaurus underneath more than once. The word the soldier used of Scaurus was *cinaedus.*"

Cinna's eyes flickered away from Helvia.

"There's no limit to what people will *say* of course," Helvia stammered, as her world tottered. "Can he be depended on to tell the truth, this man who told you?"

"Considius vouches without qualification for his truthfulness," Cinna returned.

Helvia stared aghast at him. Sexual behaviour was versatile in the Roman world, but the submissive man was a figure of shame and ridicule. Her daughter to marry that sort . . .

But she had no chance then to think, to react. A knocking and ringing shouts from the vestibule announced the return of the son of the family from Athens.

The entire household crowded excitedly around the new arrival —beloved heir and apple of his father's eye. Young Quintus had come from Athens, almost—he asserted—without having paused for breath.

He shouted for Fufidia. "Where is my darling little sister?"

"Oh, she is fussing with her dresses, with her hair, with her ornaments," said her father. "Or else she's in the bathroom— very probably in the bathroom, where all young girls spend so much time looking at themselves in the mirror. Of course you don't know the big news—she is to be married to a handsome young man of rank."

Before he had fully explained, Fufidia, as if to prove her father's words, appeared wearing the best of her new dresses with a necklace given her by Lucius Scaurus. Nowadays Fufidia might live almost in an Aemilian dream, blind to all but her fiancé, but she smiled radiantly now at her beloved brother.

"You are taller, *mi frater.* You speak louder. I heard you from . . ."

"From the bathroom!" he returned, and they all laughed.

It was charming to see his dark curly head against her fairness. Quintus was tall, still with the slenderness of an adolescent. He had his father's handsome head and dark intelligent eyes. His nose was slightly aquiline and there was a fine moulding to his face.

"He would look well in bronze," thought Gratidia. "He would stand graceful on a pedestal, his head inclined slightly, his close-set curls low on forehead and cheeks and neck." Her heart swelled.

Later in life young Quintus would have assurance with all. Now at eighteen it came and went. It left him now as he stammered with delight to see his sister.

"Fufi." It was his childhood name for her. "I must grab you before you run off to your handsome husband! What is this dress? You are *too* beautiful in it."

"I told her not to wear it today," Helvia broke in determinedly. "Her friend Marcia comes to visit with her family, and she will not be dressed as well," she explained to Quintus, trying to act normally.

"Oh, Mamma," protested Fufidia. "Marcia has a much prettier one."

Her brother stuck an attitude and declared, "You will more effectively eclipse Marcia by standing in her shade."

"That doesn't make much sense," giggled Fufidia.

"You don't like epigrams? Then you should like compliments. If you want me to praise your looks, you can have the choice of the simple Attic style, the florid medium, or the grand manner.

I've learned to wave my arms with the best of advocates and throw my voice."

"Now then," said his father. "No one can stand orators who shout out their speeches. You know what Cicero says himself: just as lame men ride on horseback because they cannot walk, so these men shout because they cannot speak. Look, I have some splendid news. Cicero has invited you for a talk and he will give you some points. You are a very lucky boy."

Quintus' eyes shone. "I'd better practise beforehand. I've a good supply of imaginary cases, at least. Here is a law, for instance: 'A husband may lawfully kill his wife's lover, provided he kills her also.' "

Helvia broke in peremptorily. "Enough, my boy. We must all go to eat now."

Her tone was severe and her son quickly responded.

When Gratidia retired after lunch to take her siesta, Helvia followed her, rather to Gratidia's surprise.

The old woman collapsed on a seat, one hand to her rump. "I am the most miserable of mortals," she groaned. "Until you suffer pain like mine, don't feel yourself too badly off. Pass me the third bottle from the right on that shelf, would you?"

"Do you want your doctor?"

"Doctors . . ." Gratidia returned gloomily. "What can they do for me? Mild pain, one drop; bad pain, two drops. Three drops if I'm dying, I suppose. *Not* the second one! *That* bottle will put me out of my misery for all time!"

"Why do you keep it with the others, then?"

"To have my escape from the pain of this life always before my eyes."

Her escape was a bottle of deadly potency. Often she had terrified the children with it in their early years.

Helvia was not listening. Suddenly she burst out. "This marriage!"

"Yes?"

Helvia stood silent, fighting with herself.

Gratidia waited a moment and said, "I see nothing but good from it. A splendid match. Fufa will become a *nobildonna*. And your husband is thinking also of his son Quintus, even before his daughter. Young Quintus is going to prove himself brilliant—look at Cicero's interest in him—and it will be good for him to have an Aemilius Scaurus as his brother-in-law. And for Fufidius as well to be able to refer to Lucius as his son-in-law." Gratidia looked thoughtfully at Helvia. "For you . . ."

"Oh yes, it follows logically—as I am to be his mother-in-law!" Helvia's tone was caustic. "I should be so proud!" She strode angrily around the room.

"Fufidius is a good man," observed Gratidia. "He does well to be proud of what he has arranged."

There was a little silence, and Gratidia added, slyly, her eyes on Helvia, "What an advocate young Quintus will make. You can see his mind and tongue working at top speed. He can thunder and he can talk soft and insinuate and sparkle. He has been well trained. Your brother Cinna would agree with me that the marriage will also be of advantage to Fufidia's brother."

There was a little silence while Gratidia pondered. "A pity," she continued, "that your brother has no son of his own."

"But I am thinking of Fufidia!" returned Helvia, in cold exasperation.

"What of Fufidia?" asked the old woman.

"I've decided the marriage is all wrong, never mind its social benefits. I want to stop it. I don't know how."

"All very sudden, isn't it? You were rather pleased with the young man only yesterday."

"Well, I'm not now."

"A good wife supports her husband," intoned Gratidia maddeningly. "You must consider it isn't good for the young to see friction between parents."

"There are things you don't know!"

"What things?"

"About Lucius Scaurus."

Gratidia waited and Helvia continued.

"At the battle of Thapsus in Africa, he did not fight. And why? Because . . . because he couldn't."

"Was he ill?"

"Not ill." Helvia spat out the words, then compressed her lips.

"You don't mean he was a deserter! That isn't possible for a man of his rank."

"Deserter or not, he managed to avoid that battle. Common soldiers were there to see him avoid it," retorted Helvia. "The night before he'd so exhausted himself with a young soldier and drunk so much wine that he couldn't even ride his horse the morning of the battle."

"Who tells you this?" asked Gratidia, with evident disbelief.

"My brother told me! And Lucius is not only heavily in debt; he is a man of the worst habits." Helvia added, in a horrified whisper, "He submits to men."

Gratidia shot a look at her and mumbled embarrassedly. At length she said slowly, "Your husband will never allow this marriage contract, which he arranged, to be broken now."

"She *can't* marry him!" Helvia cried.

"Poor little Fufidia. She can't know what's behind that handsome face. She adores him. She's bent on marrying him. She is bewitched."

Helvia started violently. "That's just it! She's bewitched. In a dream. I can't talk to her. She won't hear a thing against him. She *is* bewitched."

Gratidia swallowed the rest of her medicine, grimacing. "If Fufidia has had a spell put on her for the benefit of a young man who is bad, then this spell might be broken. Once I had toothache cured by a Marsian witch. She might be procured again." She looked searchingly at Helvia. "The Marsi can cure snakebite . . ."

"Unfortunately Fufidia has a complaint worse than toothache or snakebite." Helvia threw up her hands. "Magic!" she scoffed. Then she fell silent, staring sightlessly before her. "Magic," she repeated. "Magic . . . what would it be?"

Gratidia said gratingly, "Evil spells seek evil out."

"What's that supposed to mean?"

"I must rest now." Gratidia was sweating and shaking a little as though from fever.

Helvia walked to the door, and then turned to say, "Get that witch. Get her for me as soon as we get back to Rome. I want to know more."

Gratidia was saying to herself, sitting there on her bed, "To

miss a battle is not good. It is shameful. Yes, shameful for a man
of rank."

Her head moved from side to side as though she were arguing
with herself.

IX

Only on the surface was the family gathering a happy one, up on the cool heights of Tusculum, even if one day followed another in ordered comfort, with friends, outings and parties. For the first time in her life, Fufidia avoided her mother, sensing that something had gone wrong and that it had to do with her. Lucius Scaurus was away with his father in Campania, where they were trying to get repayment of debts owed them, so Fufidia devoted herself to her brother and their friends.

Fufidius was apprehensive. Helvia spoke to him only when necessary and with a set expression. At night, if unable to sleep, he would see her shadow passing up and down, up and down, against the alabaster screen of an interior partition. He escaped to friends in the neighborhood as much as he could, blandly disregarding his wife's obvious concern. It could only be the money that worried her. It was going to consume much of the dowry which Helvia had brought to their own marriage. Fufidius waited for her assault.

In late September the family returned to town, the procession of litters and wagons jolting slowly along the dusty Appian Way, past the imposing tombs, the cypresses and the oleanders still fully in scented flower. Down in Rome the summer had rolled on, splendid with shows and games, and they were in time for the procession celebrating the Ludi Romani in honour of Jupiter Optimus Maximus, when a medley of horses and charioteers, naked athletes and flute and lyre players dazzled the crowds. There were dancers in scarlet tunics and bronze helmets, satyrs in goatskins, Sileni in shaggy tunics. Incense invaded the air, gold and silver vessels glittered. All twelve Olympian gods honoured the procession, borne shoulder high on stretchers. Oxen were sacrificed, then came chariot racing, seven laps around the Circus Maximus.

And in Rome one evening, when Fufidius had just come home, Helvia attacked. He had entered the atrium well content with life. Thankfully, for the weather was still hot, he allowed a servant to remove his toga and he swallowed some water mixed with a little wine. Then Helvia appeared and sat down near him.

"You have had a long day."

He assented.

"Busy with your Greek studies no doubt?"

Fufidius waved a hand. He knew it was her contemptuous reference to Eucharis, and indeed his afternoon had been spent with her and not with the small number of friends with whom he occasionally spent time on a Latin translation of Theocritus.

After a moment he risked a remark.

"Fufidia is no doubt resting after yesterday's excitement."

That had been the military tournament in the Circus Maximus when two squadrons of young *nobiles* had paraded in armour on horseback, and after complicated drill movements, fought a sham battle. Lucius had taken part and Fufidia had been enraptured. Later, she had sat beside him at the chariot races, the one occasion when men and women could sit together. She was not to know how much money he had lost in misplaced bets.

"I'm sure you are proud that everyone could see her in the company of the Scauri!" said Helvia scornfully. "And next to Lucius!"

"She was so excited at the sight of Lucius in the parade and then fighting in the battle," he smiled.

"A *sham* battle fortunately," she returned drily.

He chose not to understand her and remarked, "He's a very good-looking young man."

"If you can call him a man!"

Fufidius accepted the challenge. "What are you trying to say, Helvia?"

"I suppose you don't find it strange that he returned from Africa safe and well—when hardly a Pompeian officer escaped with his life!"

"His father told me all about that," returned Fufidius coldly. "It was a simple stroke of Fortune that on the day of the battle of Thapsus Lucius was on a reconnaissance by order of Scipio himself."

"The soldiers with him got back to see the fighting. They said he was drunk."

"As if common soldiers should be believed at the expense of a man who fought in the Greek campaigns—and did so well. You know Lucius commanded a troop of horse in Greece."

"It's what a very trustworthy old man—himself a senator—let out."

"And the Senator was there in person, I suppose?"

She said nothing for a moment, and then burst out, "His habits are beyond mention!"

"I don't understand you."

"He allows . . . he acts the woman!" Her face was suddenly suffused.

He let her struggle, then, "Are you trying to say he lets men fuck him?" Deliberately he used a brutal word. *"Quid tu ais? Num fellat?"*

She glared at him speechlessly.

"I advise you not to listen to gossip. People often say these sort of things. There's hardly ever anything in it. Malice, that's all. A bit of carousing doesn't hurt a man in any case."

He gazed at her over an insurmountable distance. A woman like Helvia, closely guarded, virtuous, what could she know of a man's life outside the home? He was himself a sober and good man, but now there flashed across his mind certain occasions during his own youth—even only a few years ago in Bithynia in strange territory tasting the exotic practices of the east for a time. In memory he felt again his excitement at the mere touch of the big half-savage Nicomedes with his liquid eyes, his golden skin and his haunting charm. But it was only an episode, and might never have taken place had women been available.

Fufidius started. Helvia was talking again.

"I don't expect you to have the sensibilities of a Sappho, but you might consider that Fufa is a child still, with the innocence of a child. You'll turn her over without a thought to a . . . to a—"

He brought his fist down on the table in exasperation. Oh, she was wrong. He would never forget his daughter's face—simply radiant—whenever she saw Lucius. After all, at nearly fifteen, she was older than many girls about to marry. He had arranged marriage for her with a handsome young noble whom she adored, and who was just as obviously infatuated with her. Would Fufa worship Lucius so, if Lucius didn't know how to treat a young girl? Helvia was simply imagining problems. It was often like this with mothers of course. They wanted their daughters to marry but couldn't bear the idea when the event approached. Fufidius dismissed Helvia's outburst from his mind and began to plan his business for the next day.

In what was becoming a whirlpool about her, Fufidia was the still centre. She had long animated discussions with girl friends about the wedding ceremony, tried on the saffron cloak and flaming orange veil which survived from her own mother's marriage, and sometimes, overawed by these ceremonial trappings, reverted to the comforting familiar company of her dolls. But always she was inwardly reliving her few but enchanting meetings with Lucius Scaurus.

Her talks with her mother began to follow a regular pattern, beginning quietly with goodwill, developing into a terrible battle of wills, a stormy monologue as Helvia pleaded with her daughter to give up Lucius. Fufidia's defence was silence. Sweet and pliant all her life, in this she revealed now an adamantine hardness. Lucius, who knew so well how to charm, had possessed —so carelessly—that part of Fufidia which reason could not touch.

Helvia, leaving Fufidius now, came on her daughter making her daily sacrifice of a meal cake to the family god Lar. To that god she would dedicate her dolls before the marriage ceremony.

"Vouchsafe me your protection and approval, O Lar," Helvia heard her say. "I will give you Chloë and Lydia and Porcius and Berenice, but not before my marriage. O Lar, treat my dollies well, for I will miss them!"

Helvia, unseen, rushed to her room and flung herself down in tears. She struggled against her helplessness. She was at the mercy of the vast and capricious whims of the forces of the universe. Chance ruled. Chance had put her Fufidia, her darling, her most precious possession, at the mercy of a young scoundrel; but for Fufidia he had the bodily form of a god. With Fufidia she could do nothing. Desperate now, Helvia knew she was ready to negotiate with the demons and deities of the Underworld. But first she prayed to Isis, the goddess of compassion.

"O Goddess, o great mother of all nature, sister-wife to Osiris, you who know grief and suffering and evil and have the gift of forgiveness—give me absolution. No longer can I bear the thought of the suffering which must arise from my misdoing. Purify and strengthen me, even though I cannot perform the rites for ten days and ten nights because of my family. Help me in my designs. Help my child, my innocent girl, so young in years, and give me strength to do what must be done."

That evening Helvia and Gratidia retired early and despatched their serving women to their own quarters. But much later, in the darkness of the sleeping house, the two women received the Marsian woman recommended by Gratidia's friend. The Marsian was thin and wiry, perhaps fifty years of age, with black hypnotic eyes that, once encountered, seized and drained the viewer of resistance. Helvia found her voice unexpectedly deep, seeming to draw on powers unavailable to others. Despite her own depression and misgivings, she had to acknowledge the authority emanating from the woman. If the Marsian had a habitation at all, it was a shifting one. It had not been easy to find her. An old flower seller near the Esquiline Gate had been bribed, a cryptic message passed from mouth to mouth, word left in a certain bar. Her existence was mysterious, though it was said that she procured young men for rich ageing women, and young girls for old men. She asked Helvia for five hundred *sestertii,* and not before she had thrust the bag of money into the folds of a voluminous gown did they get down to business.

Now, following the woman's instructions, Helvia performed a *defixio* or spell. On a piece of parchment which the woman described as "hieratic" she had Helvia put a lead ring and trace the outlines, then tint the outlined area with myrrhed ink, and write certain characters inside the ring. Within the circle inside the ring she had Helvia write more magical characters and the name of Fufidia.

"Let her thoughts be bound so that she may lose her desire for her fiancé. Let her never marry him!" Helvia intoned.

With trembling hand, Helvia then put the ring on the papyrus once more and turning up the papyrus outside the ring, wrapped it up completely.

Piercing the package through the characters with the pen and tying it, she repeated after the woman, "I bind Fufidia with regard to this. Let her not speak, not be contrary, not oppose; let her not be able to look me in the face nor speak against me; let her be subjected to me, so long as this ring is buried. I bind her mind and her brains so that she may not marry him."

"Now," said the Marsian woman, "I shall take the package to the grave of someone untimely dead. I shall dig a hole four fingers deep and put it in. I shall say, 'Spirit of the dead, whoever you are, I give over Fufidia to you so that she may not marry.' Then I shall fill up the hole and go away. I shall do this when the moon is waning."

Once more the whole was repeated, with another papyrus, another ring, and with the name of Lucius Scaurus.

That was not all. Afterwards the woman produced a little box, and drew from it the body of a dead frog.

"Look," she said. "I cut open the stomach. Inside it I put a lead plate on which I had inscribed with a bronze stylus certain writing and a figure. This I smeared with blood from a bat. I stitched up the frog once more with Anubian thread and a bronze needle.

"Take this frog and hang it up at the east of your property where the sun rises. On a reed taken from your garden, hang it by means of these hairs, which come from the tip of the tail of a black ox."

Helvia's heart beat fast. "What writing is inscribed?" she asked fearfully.

"This is the meaning," replied the woman. "Supreme angels, just as this frog drips with blood and dries up, so also will the body of him, Lucius Scaurus, whom Mucia Tertia bore, because I conjure you, who are in command of fire, by the dread and sacred words Maskelli Maskello."

The woman's mysterious eyes bore into Helvia. "The spell is a powerful one. It will not fail you."

She passed her hand rapidly in front of her several times in some magical obeisance to the dark all-powerful ones, and taking the papyrus parcels, was conducted by the other two to the street door. Outside, she was rapidly swallowed up by the darkness.

X

It was very late on the third evening of the Saturnalia and the party in Eucharis' house was uproarious. Oil lamps were guttering and the fumes from braziers mingled with perfume and roasted duck. The dining room was filled with men and the hubbub of their voices. The evening had begun as a festive dinner and poetry reading, but had become a drinking party. Eucharis was still there but would probably soon retire. Tonight she had received many presents—not only the usual wax candles, but wine and cakes and flowers. Her son Pamphilus got presents too.

The gatherings in her house had sprung up by chance. As Eucharis' publishing business became better known, learned men, a few writers of mimes, poets, would drop in at her place, sometimes meet each other there and stay to talk. It was a novelty, this woman's business, and besides, Eucharis was so beautiful a woman, who knew Greek literature better than they. She made fine copies of the poems of Homer for Cinna, for Valerius Cato and for other notables. Then a full edition of Parthenios' *Erotica Pathemata,* in Greek, and then in Latin. Her clientele was expanding fast now. Only last month she had begun to sell an anthology of contemporary verse.

"You will get nothing from the book merchants down in the Vicus Tuscus or the Argiletum. Copies may sell for high prices, but you won't see any of it. Come to Eucharis. She will pay you a fair proportion." The word went round.

They began to meet from time to time in a group to try their poems out on friends, and particularly on other poets, intimately, *in ioco atque vino,* rather than recite them in porticos or baths, at the mercy of the vulgar crowd. This Saturnalia gathering mingled celebration with literary talk.

"This is to Aulus Caecina." A young poet sprang to his feet. "Tell me, you fellows, how far can I go? Aulus is damnably well off, but he's not unintelligent. How much will he swallow? He's got so much money to disgorge, this patron of mine."

To the accompaniment of appreciative chuckles, he read out a poem oily with flattery to his benefactor, beginning with a line attributing to Caecina a richly royal descent from the kings of Tarquinia.

"What do you think of my first line, Eucharis: *'Caecina atavis edite regibus:* Caecina born of a line of kings'?"

"My dear boy, when the recipient is a man, the sky *is* the limit! Why not make his descent from the gods? 'O Aulus, you whom the gods themselves are proud to call brother . . .' "

Shouts of laughter. They were all just drunk enough to be delighted with any joke at all.

"But I say, don't you think that's a little bit *too* fulsome? He's only a merchant, you know."

"Gods like merchants. They both know what money can do."

"Tell me," one young poet murmured aside to another. "What price Eucharis?"

"No price will be enough, I assure you."

"Someone told me she was a *mima.*"

"It's not referred to now. And it was a good while back. She was never in the *ludi* you know. All very exclusive. Only the best houses. And she was soon rescued."

"Eucharis?" broke in another. "Oh, she's the girl of Quintus Fufidius. The father of that boy over there. You'd better watch yourself, otherwise you'll find you're out on your ear. She belonged to Parthenios once, then to Cinna, but then Fufidius bought her and set her up here. Saserna told me he once asked Fufidius, as an old friend, for the loan of her. He found out it was absolutely not the thing."

"A pity. There's something about the way she moves. I tell you I'd pay a lot to have her."

"Be happy that she is your hostess, because she won't be your whore, *carissime.* She's special. Educated. Very high-class now."

Furius Bibaculus had lurched in very late, already rather drunk and wearing a wreath of flowers sideways. He was accompanied by a flute girl, whom Eucharis promptly ordered to be shown the door again. She allowed no woman to attend these

gatherings and herself left if things got too boisterous. Bibaculus
had wavered, then left with his girl.

Fufidius' son Quintus was there, feeling it a sort of second
début, almost a literary *toga virilis,* to be present at such a gathering, which was made all the more distinctive by the presence of
his uncle Cinna. Young Quintus felt he had been invited because
of his success in Athens. He was excited, appreciative of all the
jokes he could understand, though by now so drunk that he
contributed very little. Also there, of course, was Parthenios,
honoured hardly less than Cinna in that gathering, sensitive to
the nuances of poetry as an aspen leaf is to the breeze. There
were two of his protégés, young writers from the Greek south,
as well as Valerius Cato, instructor of young poets, the *nobilis*
Calvus, Gallus and Cornificius, son of the senator, even Asinius
Pollio shortly to govern Spain.

"Who is that pretty little child there, with the bronze-coloured
curls?"

"That's Eucharis' son. He's only eight, so don't get ideas
about him. Full of learning, too. Recites the leg off an iron pot,
so you'd better not get him started. Odious little bastard in my
opinion."

"Here, *pupe,* what's your name?" The other man beckoned
the boy over.

"Pamphilus, sir."

"What's that you've got in your hand?"

"A wooden duck, sir, filled with nuts."

"A nice present."

"From Parthenios, sir."

"Where are you off to?"

"I have to go to bed now. Mamma says, when the second
mixing bowl of wine is finished, I must go."

"Why is that?"

"It wouldn't be safe for me, sir, later on, when you all get
drunk."

"You're quite right. There is truth in wine and in children."

"Especially when the wine is from Chios," said his friend appreciatively.

For all the brilliant talk and the reading of some excellent verse, for some the evening had taken on a glamour and excitement more by reason of the presence, on the couch of honour, of a tall youth of such beauty that a scuffle almost took place for the honour of a place next to him. This was Lucius Scaurus, who wasn't at all sorry to be present. He needed the evening's festivities to banish thoughts of a bruising afternoon. This had begun with Lucius making a restrained approach to his father for more money. He wanted to appear in a good light before the Fufidii, even though the family was not of their own class. But this had only made his father round on him.

"Don't you despise the equestrian order," he told Lucius sharply. "Our links with them go back to your great-grandfather. And while my father rose to be consul, his wealth came from commerce. No need to bring it up to others now, of course."

Lucius realised that his father must have been brooding again on his own enforced departure from high public office.

Sure enough, Scaurus had gone on venomously, "I would have had a glorious career as well, but for that liar Appius Claudius. When he managed to get me tried for extortion, everyone knew it was only a dirty trick to stop me standing for the consulship." Scaurus had cursed again and then returned to his son's request. "No more money from me. And no scandals either, with this rich marriage coming up!" And he had limped from the room.

Lucius had been left despondently thinking of the presents he would still have to buy somehow and of the charm he would have to expend. And he thought irately of the girl's mother—so fair, so tall, clearly with Celtic blood in her veins—who managed to intimate, without a word, that he was inferior. Lucius was keenly and angrily aware that she obviously thought her daughter was too good for him. For a Scaurus!

There was no end to his troubles. The encounter with his father barely over, he had been stopped on his way to Eucharis' party by no fewer than four of his creditors. Again he had brought up the imminence of the date when he would get his hands on the dowry, but had been forced to agree to pay something within a few days. How, he did not yet know.

So Lucius gladly abandoned himself now to the pleasures of

drinking good wine and feeling the fervent admiration of those discerning men about him. Flushed now with immoderate drinking, he was only the more appealing. Parthenios had stuck a rose in his hair and was talking to him in a low voice—winningly.

Cinna had had a battle with Eucharis about the attendance of Lucius. She hadn't wanted him there.

"You'll allow it for my sake, won't you, Eucharis?"

"It is distasteful to me. . . . He is to marry Fufidia, no?"

"Yes. It has to do with that. I want to look him over."

She gave him a long, unfathomable look.

"I want it to be a chance encounter," coaxed Cinna. "Between the two of us."

"It would not be that. Lucius does not know anyone."

"Yes, he knows Cornificius very well."

"I do not think that Lucius Scaurus writes poetry."

"Oh, everyone writes poetry these days—or pretends to. But you look distraught, Eucharis. What is it?"

She shook her head. "I know him," she muttered. "I *hate* him."

"I think," remarked Cinna, "I am quite prepared to hate him too." After a pause, he added, "What a lot you know about everyone, Eucharis."

She shook her head, without meeting his gaze.

"I don't ask you for favours, Eucharis, and yet I have done much for you."

"Oh, you have, you have. And I am grateful."

"Then . . ."

"I will do it."

"Then I will get Cornificius to bring him along."

Cinna looked at her and said gently. "You are as lovely as the summer flowers, Eucharis. What a woman you have become. I am proud of you."

A little smile, very charming, lit her face.

"You can be so many things, Eucharis, can't you? And which is true? You are intelligent, and witty—now shy, now soft, now hard; you are innocent and very experienced. Have you a heart, Eucharis, underneath?"

It was hot now in the triclinium. The air was heavy with the sweetness of incense that Eucharis had burning. The houses in that quarter were not connected to the aqueducts and smells could be overpowering sometimes. But way of compensation, Eucharis had paid much attention to the artistic appointments of her room and her walls had been prettily painted—as a gift—by a young painter whom she knew. Charming wooden panels told stories from mythology, surrounded by delicate traceries of flowers. Against a rich red background, a frieze lower down portrayed Cupids—busy Cupids, Cupids selling flowers, making oils and perfumes, Cupids racing in chariots, acting as goldsmith, gathering grapes, running races. Cupids bewinged and playful.

"You shun me, Chloë, like a fawn . . ." declaimed a young man.

There were jeers.

"Chloë is more like a plump mare, not a fawn," cried another.

When the poem was finished, Cinna was ruthless in his versified comment:

> "Did I not love you more than my own eyes,
> I'd banish you for ever from my sight
> For dealing in such wails and groans and sighs,
> You versify so tastelessly tonight.
> The only virtue of such crap as this—
> It's copied and it's sold by Eucharis!"

The young man gasped, suddenly murderously angry at his humiliation. He lurched forward, his hand going instinctively to his dagger. Instantly Parthenios, from just behind him, brought a hand up to smack the boy smartly behind the knee. The young man doubled up and the dagger clattered to the floor.

"You'd strike a man who is master of us all?" hissed Parthenios. "Whose voice flows sweeter than honey from his tongue? Whose person is sacrosanct, even!"

The boy had collapsed on a couch. "Sacrosanct . . ." he stammered.

"Since the tenth of this month," continued Parthenios warningly. "As Tribune! Now behave yourself, little drunken one, full of black anger without reason!"

But the young poet, slumped, had begun to snore.

The floor was taken by a man called Marcius Rufus.

"It's my turn but I don't think I'll read my little piece out," he apologised. "You fellows all have rich patrons. Mine isn't rich. I must write something, just a little poem will do. Any ideas?"

"Make it a very little poem. He's such a very little man," advised Calvus slyly.

"Well, he is small, but he has a very good head. And he's been sculpted by Arkesilaos. Have you seen it? Head and shoulders only of course. Very handsome piece. It makes you think of a full-sized man."

"I've seen it. A good example of the whole being greater than the sum of the parts," retorted Calvus.

There was noisy applause. Rufus subsided rather abruptly onto his sofa. "You didn't say that, old boy. Cicero did!" he complained, then he put his head down and slept.

"All right, my friends," called Cinna. "When Rufus goes to sleep, it is time to think of breaking up. Now, have we all read our poems?" He glanced round. "Those who have not, indicate . . ."

"Our new guest has not done so," he said.

Lucius laughed deeply. Lounging there, his toga thrown back to show a comely chest and shoulders, he was flushed and glowing. "Is there a penalty for not complying?" he asked.

"A penalty? We might find a penalty for you," whispered Parthenios, and laughed, as though Lucius had made a brilliant joke.

Cinna handed Lucius a scroll. "Let us hear you read this," He commanded. "First, a drink." He signalled to a slave who filled Lucius' glass.

Lucius drained it and got to his feet, not too certainly. His wits were dulled, but the sense of well-being was strong. They were a queer lot these poets and their company, but clever-tongued. It did not hurt to be civil with them. He was wanted, he knew, by at least three of the men. All eyes were on him.

He concentrated as well as he could on the paper put in his hand. Although it was in Latin, not Greek, the poetry was too subtle and compressed for the meaning to be immediately apparent. Nevertheless, he struck an attitude and began:

"Loquacious is this youth of parts
Urged by love's fires in stops and starts.
Called up to fight on Thapsus day
Ignobly fled the other way;
Up-ended in a loving feast
Sweet thrusted by the one-back beast.

Assert your wish, the choice is yours:
Embrace great wealth? A noble cause!
Mark Julia, eager, rich and old,
Is sick; her cough is full of gold.
Let your hot passion then pursue
In wrinkled arms that death—long due;
Unless such labour is not wise—
She's willed a man of manlier size?

Seduce an infant rich in lands?
Confuse your gift with her demands?
Abandon, *cinaede,* such tender flower!
Unbind that pledge, forgo that dower.
Receive instead your kind of men—
Unite their wealth with you again,
Submission is your peak of power."

Roars of appreciation and laughter followed the reading by
Lucius Scaurus. Although what he had read was just words to
him, he joined in the laughter and drank more wine. Then the
laughter died. If Lucius had not been so drunk he would have
felt the shock and the undercurrent of tension which followed.
But for him the sofa had suddenly become better than the standing position. He felt Parthenios draw him down upon it.

Parthenios stroked his cheek. *"Submission is your peak of power.
How divine!"*

Jokes—clever and barbed jokes—were bandied round concerning the subject of the poem. They all seemed to know the
man concerned.

"He has been honoured by your reading of it," someone told
him seriously.

"Honoured . . . by my reading, was he?"

"You read it very well, Lucius Scaurus. The platform is the loser by your absence," breathed Parthenios. "There's something about the way you read—it's rich, suggestive, effective. Your voice stirs me to the depths."

"Like to meet him . . . feller in the poem. Think he's perfeckly . . . think he's guilty of something," Lucius said uncertainly.

"Why, young Lucius Scaurus." Cinna rose, facing towards him. "Why, some might say you are guilty of autobiography."

There was a sudden hush and the group fell dead still again, all eyes on the two men. Lucius reeled to his feet. The flushed faces round him were floating strangely. He was missing some meaning, he knew. What was this reference to autumn biography? Or something? He realised that he was too drunk—much too drunk—to force clarity into his understanding. Opposite him, young Quintus Fufidius' eyes bored into him, behind his mask of joviality. Lucius couldn't force order into his thoughts, damn it. Tomorrow he could do so. Yes, tomorrow. He staggered back to the couch again and the revellers, relaxed now, called for his servants to carry him off. As he went, Cinna thrust the manuscript of that poem into Lucius Scaurus' cloak.

XI

The next afternoon Lucius Scaurus sprawled indolently on the tiles of the bathhouse at the corner of the Forum while his slaves worked him over. His friend, the son of the poet Cornificius, had had Lucius carried to his own house, a short distance away from Eucharis' place. Lucius was by now feeling more his own man.

"Passed out, did I?" he enquired of Cornificius.

The other intimated that this might have been the case, airily brushing detail aside with the skill of a Cinna himself.

"What happened to the old lecher next to me?" Lucius knit his brows, trying to recall the scene of the previous night.

"Parthenios?"

"Yes, Parthenios. Careful what you're doing, you cretinous bastard!" This to his slave. "I'm not a piece of pastry!" Lucius gave a sign to the man to be off, and allowed a little boy to dress him.

"Yes, Parthenios." He smiled. "He was sorry I disappeared, I'll bet. *Perbaccho,* it was a good wine."

Bathed, oiled, dressed, restored to something like good spirits, the pair stopped at a bar a little further down the street.

"Nice position you have here, close to the baths. When I want a bath I have to go much farther."

"You're not often home, my boy."

"True. Hey, you, bring some water, quickly. I've got a simply raging thirst."

"Better not drink too much," said his friend solicitously. "Wait another bit."

"Just a little." Lucius grabbed a bread roll and some cheese. "Devilishly noisy here, isn't it? I've a filthy head. Well, I shan't have to put up with the apartment long. I'm off to Macedonia

with Ahenobarbus in the spring. Rent's appallingly high for such
a hovel. A far cry from the Palatine villa my family had once."

"It is," Cornificius agreed. "How many marble columns was
it?"

"There were three hundred and more on the theatre." Lucius
grinned. "Papa had a great many of the tallest hauled up to our
house on the Palatine. Lucullan marble. Thirty-eight feet high.
Those were the days."

"You'll have that kind of thing again."

"Oh rather," Marcus Scaurus' son returned confidently.

"There's a little apartment empty next door to me," confided
his friend. "You might use it now and then if you want. It be-
longs to my father but he is off to Africa soon as Propraetor. I
have the keys because I'm keeping an eye on it for him."

Lucius' eyes were abstracted as he munched his bread. "Seem
to remember reading out some poem or other last night."

His friend spat out an olive stone and said, looking troubled,
"You did."

"What's eating you?" demanded Lucius, feeling better now
with some food. "You look like Jupiter in a thunder cloud. If
you're worried about the money I owe you, you needn't be.
Only a matter of time before I'm in funds. Although," he continued, "if her mamma had anything to do with it, it'd be all off
with Fufidia. She hates me, Mamma does, would you believe it?
And there are great discussions at the moment about the dowry.
The father's playing very cagey with the first instalment."

"It's not that, Lucius. I know you'll soon be a rich man." From
a fold of his gown, Cornificius drew forth a roll of paper. "It's
this poem that bothers me."

"Eh? What's that?"

"You didn't know what you were reading, obviously. You
should, though."

"Was it such a winner as all that?"

"Oh, it happens to be a little work of art. In the purest iambics
as well. A difficult metre. Cinna gave it to you, so he must have
written it."

"I seem to remember I read it rather well, even though I can't
remember a thing about it. Old Parthenios told me."

As Cornificius did not reply, Lucius uttered an impatient cry and hit him playfully on the shoulder.

"What *is* the matter with you?"

"Read the poem, Lucius." His friend handed the sheet over.

"It's very involved Latin," grumbled Lucius.

"There's reference in it to several things. Thapsus for one." Cornificius was watching him closely.

Lucius spent some time with head bent over the sheet; then he said with ominous calm, "I don't think it can have been composed extempore."

"I don't either. You noticed the lines on Thapsus . . ."

"I could scarcely avoid noticing that my name is spelled out by the initial letter of each line, just to make identification doubly sure!" Lucius' face had lost all colour and he trembled now with growing fury.

"What will you do?" his friend asked nervously.

Lucius sat oblivious, seeing in his mind's eye the faces opposite him the previous night, convulsed by helpless laughter as the men rocked back and forth. His face was suddenly grotesque with hatred as he swore and dashed a jug of water to the floor. All sorts of men were in the bar. Their hubbub stopped momentarily and through jostling bodies the barkeeper pressed forward. He cringed at Lucius' expression.

"The filthy lying little upstart with his rotten verses! I'll have his guts!" Lucius said savagely. He rose abruptly.

"Let's get out of here." Cornificius tossed a coin on the counter and they pushed a way out into the narrow street. Stumbling after Lucius through the crowd, he hissed, "Wait a bit, Lucius. You've a wild look on your face I know only too well. Remember what you stand to lose."

"You'd look wild at such a gratuitous insult as that!"

"I beg you wait."

"I'm not as well as I thought I was." Lucius was shivering.

"Turn in here, then."

"Here" was the public lavatory at the intersection of the Forum and the Forum Iulium.

They sat silent for some time side by side on the resplendent marble seats. At last Lucius said sombrely, "The man's a half-wit if he thinks he can get away with it." His mouth tightened to a white line. "To ridicule an Aemilius Scaurus is a dangerous undertaking."

"Cinna is not only a tribune now," Cornificius reminded him nervously. "He's Caesar's friend. A wrong step could ruin you—and all your family."

Lucius did not reply, and Cornificius demanded, "What will you do?"

"Oh," Lucius replied, after a moment. "It'll be a pleasure to decide just *what* I'll do, *carissime.*"

It was warm and friendly in the *forica,* with the rumble of men's voices from the semicircle, the sound of running water from below mingling with the water which plashed over the dolphins in the marble fountain, executed by a Greek sculptor with such finesse. That goddess who bestows health and happiness gazed serenely down on them from on high, and raw nerves were a little calmed.

But Lucius Scaurus repeated quietly, almost to himself, "It'll be a pleasure!"

XII

"Lucius Scaurus . . ." Young Quintus murmured reflectively, as he and his father walked, under a flawless blue sky, through the cramped streets of the capital on their way to Cicero's house. "He cuts quite a dash, doesn't he?"

His father was busy seeing and being seen and did not immediately respond. Their progression was slow. They stopped frequently to talk to people and only when nearing their destination shook off the not inconsiderable retinue of Fufidius' clients. All knew where they were heading for.

"The way he lives it up won't appeal to Fufidia, Papa. He was at Eucharis' place last night."

"Did *she* stay on for the celebration?"

"Only for the beginning."

"I don't know what you mean by 'live it up'—no more than you did in Athens, judging by the money I've had to fork out over the last two years!"

Quintus knew it wasn't a very serious complaint; his father would have been positively worried if his son had not "grown up a man" and indulged himself sometimes. Quintus thought carefully.

"Not everyone at Eucharis' place was very taken with Lucius."

Fufidius dismissed this with a wave of his hand. "Poets and all that lot . . ."

"Uncle *Cinna* doesn't like him."

Fufidius said heavily, "He doesn't? And why not?"

Quintus almost dared to tell him about the poem, but instead he only muttered, "Oh, I don't know."

"Just between ourselves, your uncle is a strange man. Closed and self-contained to the point of unnaturalness. So devious you never know where you are with him."

"He's a brilliant poet, Papa."

"I'm not saying he isn't. He is your mother's favourite, but I'm never really comfortable when he's around. You always feel you're under observation. Says little but watches everything. And when he does say something, he's got a very cruel tongue. Of course, if you're one of Caesar's favourites, you can afford to talk out. Yes, what were you about to say?"

"Nothing, Papa." But after a moment Quintus added cautiously, *"I* don't like Lucius Scaurus any more than he does."

"Who's been talking to you about him? Your uncle?"

"No, Papa! Only . . ."

"Don't *you* start criticising Lucius Scaurus to me! I'm well satisfied with this marriage. D'you think Ahenobarbus would have greeted me just now if we weren't already a rung or two higher on the social ladder? *You* have your career to make as advocate. It's hardly going to hurt you to be seen passing the time of day with Lucius' future commander any more than having it known that Cicero has taken you up. Now don't forget to tell Cicero something of your experiences in Athens. His own son is probably off to Greece in the spring and he'll be interested."

They had finally reached the north side of the Palatine Hill, site of the famous villa. Destroyed by Clodius after Cicero's banishment, it had subsequently been rebuilt at the public expense. They walked up in the intimidating grandeur of flight on flight of steps leading right, then left, to the enormous terrace, where a jungle of handsome travertine columns surrounded the portico. Below, the Forum glistened in the sunlight. As Cicero said, he lived in sight of the whole city.

From this heady summit, young Quintus no longer felt quite so confident. Groups of clients waited, posturing and lording it over each other, the sound of their self-assertiveness bouncing back from marble-faced walls and floor.

"All as ready to praise Caesar today," commented Fufidius, "as they were ready to damn him yesterday."

"Cicero will never have time for us!" whispered his son.

They sent in their names and were conducted to an anteroom full of Greek statues. Cicero did not fail them. After less than an hour he received them in his library, which opened onto a covered courtyard where fauns and satyrs sported in barbaric marble elegance.

Formally attired, Cicero was still very good-looking at sixty-two. Underlying his dignity, they felt immediately the tremendous vitality of that challenging, restless intelligence. He came directly from his philosophical writings, he explained, and welcomed them warmly. Young Quintus, despite his nervousness, acquitted himself well. His father smiled at the delicate compliments his son inserted in his answers to Cicero's questions, referring to the value of the great man's writings and translations for the Romans, who had no Academy as there was at Athens and—even now—only the beginnings of a public library.

After the boy had declaimed a set piece and Cicero had made him talk about Athens, it was clear that there was something in the youth that appealed strongly to Cicero.

"Never say a great man cannot be the soul of courtesy," declared Fufidius later to Gratidia. "People talk so much of his conceit, his virulent wit and uncertain temper. To us he was kindness itself. He made jokes to put our boy at ease. It was a pleasure to see them together. Both good-looking men, one nearing the end of a glorious career, Quintus—let us hope and pray—at the start.

"Cicero gave us quite a little lecture on public speaking: 'When pleading, your first care is to be heard,' he said. 'You'll speak out in the open in all weathers; you will have to convince a jury fifty strong, and impress a motley throng of spectators. You must drive your points home over and over again—but conceal the fact that you're doing it. You must be balanced, elegant, rhythmical. You will use all manner of different styles. The grand style, for instance, to summon up the great men of the past . . . To hurl condemnation or urge right-doing, your lungs need to be strong, your speech crackling. You will have one style for the client who is renowned, another for his inferior . . . You must be master of everything—of vituperation, wit, eulogy, thunderous rage, the highest sentiments. And when your audience hangs rapt on your words, in silence absolute, you will taste power—power, moreover, for good or for evil. Politics may be dead or muffled nowadays, but this power—never!

'Remember one other thing, your case is what you make of it. Deal only with those facts you want to deal with; leave aside the unwanted or embarrassing. The least convenient sort of evidence may be twisted to your support if only you are dextrous enough. And finally, it is authority above all else that will carry your jury with you. . . .' "

As they left, young Quintus was on fire with excitement, dreaming of a great career. Trained by the master, pleading in the most momentous of cases, holding spellbound whole crowds who had come to jeer but remained to applaud.

Elated, father and son walked for some time. Up on the Palatine one breathed another air, a purer air that money bought, far from the sweat and thunder of the Circus to the south, the groaning *insulae* of the slums, the vice and suffering and tragedy of the poor and enslaved. Today the winter sun touched the grandeur of basilica and portico to a dull gold. A noble view—indeed, the view of nobles.

In a little street of the same name stood the Temple to Fortune of this Day. They went in to make a timely offering to the Goddess. Fufidius was delighted to walk with his son like this, thinking back some few years, when he had first come to Rome and established his family there. He had given young Quintus over to highly recommended teachers, but he himself had taken the boy everywhere.

They parted at the bottom of the steps leading down from the Palatine, which ended at the sacred Spring of Juturna. There, too, they were careful to throw some coins in the fountain. Then the father turned towards the neighbourhood of Carinae, and Quintus took the Via Sacra by the old Basilica Sempronia. Behind scaffolding an army of workmen were transforming it into the Basilica Iulia. In the shops alongside it Quintus spent some time looking for a gift to please his sister, so soon to marry that boy whom he had seen the night before for only the third time and who had reclined indolent and amused opposite him. Again the question hammered him: was it really true what they had said about Lucius Scaurus last night? Uncle Cinna had ridiculed him mercilessly. Of course, Uncle Cinna had always been devoted to Fufidia. His mother, too. Quintus himself was his father's boy, everyone said. It had always been like that.

He put these thoughts from him. He was on his way now to a rehearsal of Plautus' *Mostellaria* with his friend Publius Lucilius

Longus, son of a senator from Aricia. The rehearsal was in a theatre in the Campus Martius. The excitement of the morning still pulsed hot in Quintus, however. He would have liked to savour it alone, this exhilaration, for underneath there was the quaking dread that he might not measure up. To expend some of this tension he needed a girl, but he had never had the confidence to visit a brothel alone. Perhaps Publius would go with him, after the rehearsal.

When Publius arrived, he talked steadily.

"When this theatre was dedicated, five hundred lions and elephants were slaughtered. My father brought me. But the crowd didn't like it, you know. Neither did I. I was only eight years old then. It was the elephants that were worst. I'd sooner watch a play, you see, or something amusing. I expect this theatre is as good as any you've seen in Athens. And the play is one of ours!"

"One of ours," agreed Quintus. "But the story is Greek, the flavour Greek." He laughed. "And in Greece you don't have to call a theatre a temple when you build it."

At the end of the first act a mime was put on. A curtain was run across the stage and a fat fellow sauntered out to beseech their attention. His wife was in there—he gestured—and he wanted to go out and keep an appointment with a girl. What could he do? He spoke roughly, in the vulgar language of the people. A delighted cry came from the pit, though it was only from stagehands. A girl pranced on stage from time to time and there was a great deal of horseplay behind the wife's back. Amazing that she could not see it. For the benefit of the spectators, the fat man managed to strip the girl of most of her clothes.

Quintus said, "Let's go to that brothel in the Clivus Suburanus afterwards, shall we?"

"I can't," returned Publius. "I'm tied up for the rest of today. My father has important guests."

Quintus decided to walk home. It was not yet quite dark, though shops were closing and houses shuttered. He turned towards the Forum, leaving behind the grandious complex of theatre, temple and porticoed art gallery. He entered mean little alleys. People jostled him. Here were sickening smells and rough language. His was the only toga in sight. He thought of the slaughter of all those beasts in that very theatre and he thought of the woman in the mime. Coarse and provocative. He thought of Cicero and wondered if he, as a young man, had had many girls. Quintus did not think so, somehow. He doubted if Cicero much liked women. Excitement returned now. Cicero was so much the master of fine words, without which there could be no reason, no subtlety of thought, no refinement, no intellectual life, in fact, no life worth living. Listening to the uncouth mouthings around him, he was convinced that words were the very quality of life. He strode on.

The little patch of sky between tall houses was darkening fast now. A woman came towards him and stopped, turned side on and flattened herself against the wall, tilting her head invitingly. Then he saw the smile freeze on her face and her eyes widen. Instinctively he sensed danger. At that moment someone pushed Quintus roughly from behind. He staggered and would have fallen if a dark figure had not shot up from nowhere and caught him. Then his arms were gripped on both sides and he was hurried along in the shadow. There was hardly time for fear.

"Don't struggle," said a voice. "It's no use. Keep walking."

Quintus could quite see it was no use. In this area he could expect no help. For a little he could not quite believe what was happening. Violently, he was half dragged, half propelled along. He felt the force of the big man who was digging his fingers into him. Terror rose in him then. There seemed to be three of them, rough men, perhaps slaves. They kept to the little alleys and to mean streets which Quintus did not know. At last they stopped, in a wider street, also unknown to him. There was just enough light for one of the men to turn a key in a lock and open a grating in a wall. Quintus thought the big man was a black. He stumbled in and was hustled across a courtyard and up some narrow stairs. He could not speak for fear, and trembling, hated himself for it.

Inside a room—to his surprise it seemed a presentable room, no doubt part of a well-to-do house—one of his assailants lit an oil lamp and he saw them properly for the first time. Three men. The big black, probably a Numidian, the other two perhaps also of foreign extraction. The man in command had a vicious, twisted face. The black man looked slow-witted and made strange sounds. The third man was short but strongly built. He seemed half scared, half rapturous. He came up to Quintus and put a hand on him, feeling his body.

At this gesture, revulsion rose in Quintus and he sprang back. "Take your hands off me! Take my money if you want." He threw down the few coins he was carrying. "You'll get nothing else."

The giant black cuffed him over the head. Quintus felt the strength of that glancing blow.

Then the first man said, "You'll be good."

He came up to Quintus and unfastened his toga and stripped him. With the black man in close support, he began to throw Quintus around and then to paw him. The youth struggled and shouted to him to stop. The man's breath was on him. Quintus struggled harder but the man's intentions were unmistakable. Suddenly the boy brought his knee up. The other loosened his grip and staggered back, screaming with rage and pain. The black man punched Quintus in the head and chest and grasped his arms. He forced him over a wooden seat and held him there. Then the first man, recovered, picked something up, and bringing his hand down, made the air crack. Quintus felt the lash of a whip. It hissed and cut, hissed and cut, cut fire into him.

"Give it him good. He's never been hit in his life. Look at his white skin." The short man slobbered.

"Now you know . . . what it's like. Now you know . . ."

Rhythmically, the first man lashed the bared torso of the youth.

The other two laughed, watching the scene with enjoyment. The short one giggled, his mouth dribbling.

"He's smooth and tender like a baby. Master said not to scar him too much."

"Scar him? With this little thong? He likes it. Don't you, little one?" He made the thong swish horribly.

Quintus seemed to taste blood, the blood from his body. The pain was searing and ever exacerbated. But the men laughed.

At a specially vicious lash he slipped to the floor and the little man rushed towards him. Quintus felt the second man grab him from the other side. They fought over him, pulled at his legs, held him.

Then one said, "We'll give Maurus first turn. Because he has no tongue and can't speak. Did you know that, little one? He was in the mines, and he saw something he shouldn't and they cut his tongue out."

They held Quintus down. And the man penetrated him. They took turns. Shame and pain blended, with something even more humiliating, a searing heat that might have been ecstasy.

He fell to the ground, ruptured and bleeding.

"A high price has been paid for a poem, hasn't it?"

A voice came from the darkness. *"You* won't read any poems by your uncle in a gathering, will you, Quintus Fufidius? And what ignominy for all your family if it were known that slaves had ridden you! Take your toga and go your way. The door is open."

One of the men threw some water over Quintus. The youth struggled to his feet as best he could. His toga was thrown over his violated body and he was pushed from the room, down the steps, across the courtyard, out into the night.

To his surprise, a litter awaited him outside. He stumbled into it and heard someone give directions to the bearers to take him to his own apartment. There, they unceremoniously tipped him out by his father's door and fled.

The doorman noticed nothing wrong as he let Quintus through the iron grille. Quintus half crept, half reeled across an atrium empty but for two sleeping slaves.

The statue of the family god Lar, under which a little oil lamp continuously burned, grinned jovially at him, emphatic reminder that here Quintus was again in the bosom of a close-knit family.

"Not one of them will ever know," his nauseated brain cried out. "No one will ever know." He had reached this essential conclusion instinctively and surely. "My shame will be mine . . . And revenge on that filthy two-faced scum will be mine . . ."

The Lar smiled ever more encouragingly.

"There's no shame in it," part of his mind told him. "You must tell your father so he can save Fufa from this marriage."

"Tell him and he'll be forced to kill Lucius Scaurus," came the

response. "And then the whole family will bear the conse-
quences."

Rage—burning rage—overpowered him then.

"I'll handle this myself," vowed young Quintus. He crept to
the door of his room. Inside a lamp burned and a half-sleeping
Gratidia grunted, rubbed her eyes and struggled up to greet
him.

XIII

Eucharis was about to take a bath—a ceremonial bath. Today she would begin the first of her *puri dies* or pure days, ten of them, when she would spend ten successive nights in the temple of the goddess Isis, and perform the rites of chastity.

At first light, water-carriers had already been trudging to and fro with their jars, servants had been despatched to the *tinctor* or cleaner for the newly laundered clothes—of course to find them not quite ready, which meant all had been held up in the meantime. Finally Eucharis stood in place on the gently sloping stone floor of her little bathroom with the grating in the centre of the floor. Her two personal maids poured water from pitchers and sponged their mistress' beautiful body. Honey and almond oil was rubbed into her skin. Her hair was washed, combed and dextrously dressed. Essences and perfumes were applied. At last, after frantic demands, a spotless dress was carried home from the cleaners, laid out ready and donned. There remained only the *stola,* which would be ready in one hour more.

As the household worked, it talked—more or less continuously—and the scrape of sandals on tiled or stone floor never ceased. The hubbub—at times violent, at times playful—gave flavour and excitement to the morning.

"You've put on the beans without soaking them first. They'll break up. Have you never heard of soaking beans overnight?" The fat cook stood over a little slave girl. "And now you are cooking them without onions. May Cerberus savage you with his dread jaws before you even reach hell!"

Meanwhile, ashes were removed from braziers, chamber pots emptied, refuse carted away. In the midst of it all a note arrived for Eucharis which negated her day and threatened the household with confusion.

"Set out two chairs and do the floor in my room. Also my

bedroom. I have to receive a visitor," she explained hurriedly to her favourite servant. "And send that sniggering fool off," she added angrily to another. "If I catch her with that expression on her face again, she'll go without food for a week."

This was done. The note was curt and peremptory, as Marcus Scaurus had so frequently been. He would not have cared in the slightest if he had known that this note, like others conveying a like message, had been shown by the slave who carried it to his son Lucius, who made it his business to be abreast of the private lives of his family and friends. The note said:

"I beg you to be at home and at leisure at the ninth hour, when I shall visit you. Also to have available that room where you have received me before. And to occupy your family in duties which will take them far off."

Tears of mortification welled for a moment. Eucharis was a *domina* now, yet these notes—orders, rather—were worded so as to reduce her to the girl of five years before, when she had danced to please men, and had pleased Marcus Scaurus in bed.

With a resigned sigh, she rearranged her afternoon. She had the women feed Pamphilus, who had just got back from school, and sent him to bed for his siesta. A slave was sent scurrying for delicacies to the pastry cook. Sawdust was thrown afresh on the floor and brooms applied. Once more Eucharis changed her clothes and arranged her hair. And then sent her staff off to their own quarters.

Soon afterwards her visitor arrived. He came in a closed litter which was left two streets away. As was understood between them, no person saw him enter but Eucharis. He stood over her in a proprietorial way.

"You get prettier with the years." Marcus Scaurus peered into her face. "Eh? What's this? Not glad to see me?"

Eucharis feigned pleasure which did not deceive him.

"It's that accursed goddess of yours. Don't flinch! I've told you before she won't do you any good. Why have the shrines been done away with so many times? Because these imported gods are bad. Isis! Dogs and cats! What do you all get up to in the temple? I bet you make assignations." He made various indecent suggestions.

"Oh no! It is not true!"

"Then you certainly waste money. They are bound to be after the money of their devotees."

"Sometimes one donates a little money—or some food."

"A nice fat goose? Anubis must get a lot out of you and your like. What do you give? A goose? Or a *volumen?*"

He sneered and threw some money down. Eucharis noted that it was not much.

"But a dress instead. And now," he grasped her. "You know what I want." He whispered something in her ear.

"Not a goose or a *volumen.*"

Her tone was sulky. She twisted from his arms and walked away. He liked her rude and hard. She owed it to him to be what he wanted, now and then. As he often said, he had done a lot for her when she was a *mima.* His attentions had led to those of other men and had earned her money. But Eucharis was afraid of him—no less now than when he had thrown his money around. He pulled her to him, intent and stern-faced. Then he began trembling. But Eucharis knew what was needed. She had developed during the days of her work as a mime, and had many and various arts. She knew what to say now—and what to do. What Scaurus had come for would soon be achieved.

Finally, that evening, after another hasty and secret bath, Eucharis, clad once more in her clean dress and *stola,* took her place among the throng of worshippers in the colonnaded precincts of the temple of Isis. It was in the Campus Martius, for Isis had four times been banished from the centre of the city. The goddess always reappeared, however. Not too many years ago the Consul Lucius Aemilius Paullus had had to seize an axe himself and give the first blow to the temple doors since no workman dared to begin the work of destruction. For Isis appealed to all—to the downtrodden or poor as well as the high-born and wealthy. Her worshippers swayed now in sacred dance and chanted the responses. All things to all men was Isis, goddess of chastity, goddess of fertility as well. Good and kindly, she prevailed through love and compassion.

Priests clothed in linen unveiled the sacred image of Isis and her husband/brother Osiris, who were dressed in holy garb and adorned with jewels and vultures' feathers. Priests and priest-

esses sprinkled each member of the congregation with holy water from the Nile. They lighted tapers for the evening service.
Only let Eucharis keep faith, only let her follow the sacred rites,
and Isis would bring to her both money and advancement.

On her way to the temple, Eucharis had taken the Clivus Pub-
licius that led to the Aventine or Hill of Diana. It was in Diana's
temple that she had first taken refuge, years before, when she
had run away from the Fadii with her baby. Ever since, on the
13th of August, when Diana decreed a holiday for slaves, Eucharis washed her hair and joined in her worship. She never made
her way to the temple of Isis without first paying her respects to
Diana who stood on the Aventine, a pretty little wooden statue
from Ephesus. Isis could enter any other goddess and so Isis and
Diana were one and the same. But it was well to take no risks in
the matter.

The singing swelled, the tapers flickered, the temple stood
splendidly illumined.

"O Goddess," prayed Eucharis. "I am in great fear and per-
plexity. Make it so that I may still have the money from my
master Fufidius. Let me continue to please him. O Goddess, I
have always been as faithful to Fufidius as I can be. You—who
know all—know that I am more deserving to be his wife than
Helvia, who has sinned. Let Fufidius adopt our son; let Helvia
who is wicked die of ten diseases, and above all let me not be
discovered in my favours to Marcus Scaurus. And let Lucius
Scaurus be stricken by mortal disease; if not that, by a hostile
sword, and die before he extorts more money from me to keep
my master Fufidius from hearing bad things of me."

As an afterthought, Eucharis added to her prayer, "Let Helvia
be stricken with baldness before she dies. Oh, let her lose at least
the front part of her hair, and let it grow thin all over and her
head be all visible at the top."

The dancers turned and dipped and slowly twirled in solemn
obeisance. Eucharis looked along the length of her own out-
stretched arm and beheld—very near—a tall woman with intent
face and fervent eyes, who stately swayed in the dance. Eucharis
twirled and after an obeisance looked once more. The woman,

lost to everything but the goddess, revolved, and Eucharis knew for sure it was Helvia. Oh, was this not a sign? Was it not in answer to her prayer? Would the goddess not tell her how to accomplish her aim?

XIV

On the January morning which none of the Fufidii or the Scauri would ever forget, Fufidius stood reviewing with Helvia the arrangements for the pre-nuptial banquet which they were to give later that day. Many relatives of both families would attend. Helvia was withdrawn these days, but Fufidius thought she seemed more resigned. She might be unaccountably opposed to the marriage, but at least she was attending to the arrangements.

As part of the entertainment for this banquet she had insisted on having a poetry reading of the *Peleus and Thetis* by Catullus.

"It's so long," he had protested. "Your audience will get bored. And is the subject suitable? A girl deceived and betrayed? At least a good part of it is taken up with Ariadne's betrayal, anyway."

"Exquisite poetry, though."

"Isn't all that food enough?" he grumbled. "Why Catullus? I was brought up on Ennius."

Despite her effort to be composed, Helvia's words were wrenched out of her.

"Catullus understood young girls. He understood what marriage means for them. He was like a woman. No ordinary man can understand what a young girl feels. Our daughters are still children when they marry. Have you ever considered it?"

Fufidius gaped at her.

"Fufa is overjoyed to marry. Every girl thinks only of marriage. It is natural. What else is there?"

Helvia bowed her head.

That same morning, in another part of the city, Eucharis was supervising the buying of vegetables in the covered market by the Porta Carmentalis. She was not happy either. The goddess Isis had brought limited comfort—added strength to bear her troubles perhaps, but not the prayed-for intercession, the firm benefits she wanted. Eucharis knew the wedding preparations went on; the marriage would be celebrated, the dowry paid, while Fufidius still kept her short of money. Her own son's chances seemed forever ruined. That, at least, was how she saw the situation.

Then she met a slave from Fufidius' family, well known to her from her own former days as a trusted member of the family. She had much to tell Eucharis of the wedding and of a dreadful commotion she had overheard.

"The master lost his temper completely. It was terrible to hear." The middle-aged woman with the lined face was slow-witted but reliable. "And it was because of the magic—"

"The magic?" Eucharis' heart jumped.

"The master found something. Hanging on a pine tree in the garden. It was the merest chance he found it, for it might have stayed there for months and no one the wiser. It was quite covered by pine needles. But the master was walking in the garden the other afternoon, as he sometimes does. It was bright sun and he was up and down, up and down, deep in thought. Then Theophilis—you know he is one of the master's personal slaves—said to him, 'Master, there is something you should see here. It is in the tree.' He was so frightened he laughed as he said it—for nervousness. Master went to the tree. It was terrible. It makes me faint to think of it."

The woman liked a good story. Eucharis, getting impatient, prompted her.

"Tell me! We will never finish our shopping otherwise."

"A little dead thing, no bigger than your palm, hanging by a reed. A little dead frog."

"A dead frog," repeated Eucharis slowly.

"A dead frog, with its stomach sewn. . . . The master looked at it and cursed horribly. Never had anyone seen him angry like that. 'Who put that object in the tree?' he shouted. 'Who?' Theophilus said he didn't know.

" 'You don't know what it is?' Master was almost raving. 'It's a magic spell. I can tell from the look on your face that you know all about it.' Theophilus insisted that he didn't. But master had him tied up and whipped. Because Theophilus was laughing for fear, still. And yet when he fell to the ground insensible, he had still not said who it was. Perhaps he didn't know. Master assembled all the slaves and said he would whip them all if they did not tell him who had done it. He said he would give them till that night. But that night came and nothing happened. Master had closed himself up in his apartment. But Tranio told me—he who is always with the master—that . . ." the woman's voice sank, "that inside the frog was writing, in the *domina*'s hand. In *Helvia*'s hand." The woman's face was lewd in its enjoyment. "And the curse was against the fiancé of the *Domina*'s daughter Fufidia—against Lucius Scaurus."

Nothing could have pleased Eucharis more. She gave the woman two *denarii* and bought her a honey cake, so pleased she was. And, much lighter of heart, she made her way home. Were her prayers at last bearing fruit?

She found the elegant young Furius Bibaculus waiting in her salon. He was throwing her dice to while away the time.

"It's a good morning for me. Eight out of ten times I have won," he greeted her. "If you will offer me wine, Eucharis, then I will tell you my requirements."

She offered—and he accepted and drank with pleasure—her good Alban wine.

"You keep a good table wine. I give you two poems to copy. I want five copies of each. Tomorrow I leave for Africa Nova with Quintus Cornificius. I am letting you have much time for the copies. Who knows when I will be back in Rome? One poem of importance is the epic on Caesar's campaign. After you have finished, please give them both to Cinna. Nice copies, if you please, Eucharis."

Bibaculus was a talker and a gossip and he drank to live up to his name. He it was who had lurched in late the night of the Saturnalia with the flute girl—and immediately been sent away. Eucharis could not make him see now that it was time to leave.

Unexpectedly, a clatter outside announced a visitor—for Eucharis, a visitor who struck fear into her. Lucius Scaurus, oiled, combed, perfumed and elegantly clad. Bibaculus still stayed on. He did not know Lucius, for he had not stayed long enough the night of the Saturnalia to talk to him, but he knew about him. He made it his business to know about people. And he talked interminably. Perhaps, though Eucharis, Scaurus might get tired of him and leave.

She sat there, listening to the one-sided conversation of the two young men. She prayed now that Bibaculus would not, after all, go. Lucius obviously wanted her alone and he wanted Bibaculus gone, but he could not on this occasion be too brutal and rude about it. Bibaculus was not a nobody. As was natural, he talked of Africa, and Lucius, reminded of the distasteful Thapsus campaign, parried his questions. Eucharis sat there full of hatred which she knew how to conceal. She knew that Lucius was accustomed to rely on his charm to get what he wanted and that he was utterly indifferent to how he used others. From an unambiguous remark to her in the atrium as he entered, she knew now she was to pay once more for his silence about his father's visits to her. She sat there and waited, her brain racing.

Lucius lounged on a couch, toying with a beautiful dice-box which he had picked up from a low table. It was in the form of a tower, with a band of diamonds at its base and top. His well-shaped and tapering fingers mesmerised the others. His whole body was appealing. He rattled the dice in the box and threw onto the table.

"Sixes!" he exclaimed triumphantly. *"Iactus Venereus!* The Venus throw! I breathed my Fufidia's name and she brought me luck. I am on my way to their banquet."

Eucharis then brought Lucius a different wine from another room. It was from Vesuvius, she said.

"I need luck today," Lucius cried, "for the banquet of the Fufidii. All the relatives will be there, on both sides." He smiled and drank. "I need strength, as the guest of honour."

Bibaculus threw in his turn. A two and three. Lucius threw a five and six.

"Ah, it's only playing for money that gives spice to it, though." Lucius' eyes were on Eucharis. "But my father keeps me very short."

"I trust your father is still in good health?" Bibaculus asked politely.

"Yes, indeed, he is very well. As active as any young man half his age," smiled Lucius Scaurus. His eyes flickered once more to Eucharis and held hers.

Eucharis hesitated and then said, as if continuing a conversation, "All women adore jewels and the like for their beauty, but I suppose that men are sometimes forced to be more practical and to think of their value and what may be bought with them." Her eyes went to the dice-box.

Lucius held the dice-box up to the light and his fingers caressed the diamonds.

"Sappho wrote of the still, hot passion of a flawless diamond," said Furius Bibaculus, who wanted to contribute elegantly to this conversation which he now found puzzling.

Lucius' eyes sought Eucharis' once more.

"Awaiting the touch of Venus for release!" he cried. "Let us dice once more."

Again they threw the dice and again Lucius turned up sixes.

"And Venus obliges!" Lucius exclaimed. "We have won, these playthings and I! Have we not?" He turned to Eucharis.

She nodded, and shortly afterwards, the two young men took their leave. Unseen by Furius, Lucius slipped box and dice into his toga pocket.

On his way to his father's, Lucius Scaurus turned into a little alley off the street of the sandalmakers, and stopped at a certain shop which he knew, of old. There he showed the dice-box to a man well practised in the art of valuation. The man named a sum. Lucius objected. The figure was raised, fractionally.

"Wouldn't you like to throw the dice just once more?" asked the man.

Lucius' hand closed on the box. He threw.

The man started. "Three aces. *Jactus damnosus!*" he exclaimed. "The worst of throws! Try again."

Lucius did so. Again three aces. Both men paled.

The pawnbroker pushed the box back to Lucius. "Go, go quickly. Find an altar and sacrifice. The gods are angry, young master!"

Lucius took up the box, and at another three aces, left the shop cursing. To restore himself, he visited a wine bar, drank and returned to the family home without sacrificing.

XV

Lucius sprang from his litter and followed his father into the atrium of the Fufidii villa on the Esquiline, where a procession of carriages had deposited the numerous family party of the Scauri. Slaves materialised about them.

As the assembled clan began to move across the gleaming travertine slabs of the atrium, laughter rose within Lucius.

"Battle stations, by Jupiter!" he breathed to himself, pacing with his father at the head of this solid phalanx of the Aemilii Scauri as they advanced towards their hosts without breaking ranks, their attitude part hauteur, part a condescending graciousness. As greetings and introductions got under way, there arose a refined murmuring of the Aemilian ladies as they gazed appraisingly around. Lucius knew to a nicety what they were thinking. They had known better than this. So few years ago, they had lived in the luxury of riches carelessly squandered by the head of their clan. All the same, they had ungrudging appreciation, these days, of less spectacular but solid wealth. And all were prepared to do justice to the meal.

While the Fufidii house did not reach the level of villa that the Aemilii Scauri would think appropriate to their standing, it was nevertheless an excellent town house, enclosed by high blank walls at street level, where the family were private and safe from the street noise outside. In summer they sheltered behind the thick stone of the walls in the enclosed garden of the central atrium and in the complex of rooms leading off it at the sides. Beyond was the salon and other rooms and a pretty garden. Fufidius had added a Greek peristyle and another lofty dining room. The walls had been decorated with great artistry and those of the triclinium gleamed with green plants, burgeoning fruit trees, a country landscape shimmering into the distance beneath a painted blue sky. Bright figures from myth sprang from artful panels. At one end the room leapt its physical boundaries, and painted columns and cornice, stuccoed architrave and portal offered a richly coloured stage set. It would be against this little masterpiece of *trompe-l'oeil* that Helvia's actors would perform.

Lucius noted young Quintus standing behind the others. He did not present himself. The uncle wasn't yet there. Lucius' lips curled contemptuously. Neat and savagely satisfying that countermove of his had been, putting this crowd in its place. But now he set out to charm, bowing engagingly to the older ladies, exerting himself for Helvia and Gratidia, who stood there richly though decorously dressed, wearing all their rings. As usual, Helvia scarcely looked at him.

But underneath Lucius was still preoccupied. His hand closed on the jewelled dice-box in his pocket. Wine had not banished the terror instilled in him by the ominous throws in the pawnshop. He looked at Fufidia, beautiful in the amber light, measuring her in terms of ready cash and percentages, finding her wanting only as a source of immediate financial solace.

He heard Gratidia remark to Marcus Scaurus, "The young man is pale. He looks wan."

And he felt Helvia's keen glance on him at last.

"He enjoys himself too well, that's the reason," returned Scaurus.

"The young ones are often less robust than the old," asserted Gratidia.

"You could be right," thought Lucius, looking at the line of the old woman's conspicuous jaw.

"They don't get gout though." Marcus Scaurus stretched with difficulty on his couch. "This foot of mine makes me pale enough. And age doesn't seem to make me more robust." He surveyed Gratidia's grimace as she settled herself. "Of course I know ladies don't get the gout," he said ironically.

"It is rheumatism," replied Gratidia briefly. She liked to think her secret drinking was not known. This evening she was careful not to touch wine.

The dining room was ablaze with expensive flowers. The silver was highly polished. The party, twenty-seven in all, settled down on clusters of richly covered couches, three diners to a couch, set round three large and finely inlaid marble tables. It

was a daring move for the Fufidii to have the ladies recline with
the men instead of sitting upright and apart. Beforehand, there
had been heated arguments on the matter. Gratidia had been
shocked.

"Only loose women recline with the men," she complained.
"I have never seen it done before."

"It is often done at elegant gatherings," Fufidius explained.
"The Scauri will be used to this sort of thing."

So Fufidius had Marcus Scaurus on his left, Helvia on his right.
Fufidia and Lucius shared the couch on the left together with
Marcus Scaurus' wife, a plain, good, long-suffering woman rarely
seen in public. She was his fourth wife, her estate he had long
since gone through. Gratidia shared the couch on Helvia's right
with two elderly Aemilian aunts.

The dinner was splendid—perfectly cooked, served by well-
trained slaves. There were no peacocks or lampreys, but Caesar's
sumptuary law was strained. They began with oysters—large suc-
culent oysters from Circaeum, and went on to mullet, then delicately flavoured roast veal. Vegetables and salads abounded, and
pastries and fruits. The wine was from Falernum.

For Fufidius it was a joyous occasion. He was proud to have
Marcus Scaurus beside him and to see the Scauri eat his food. He
and Scaurus got on easily enough. Scaurus talked of Lucius' com-
mission on the staff of Ahenobarbus.

"He'll be off very shortly, once the marriage is over. I wonder
if this famous invasion of Parthia will come about. I don't like
what I hear these days. The sooner Caesar gets away the better.
Seems to be working his own ruin here, or cooking his own
goose if you like—smothered with regal honours?"

Helvia, not being required to take part in this conversation
and giving scant attention to the ladies on her right, brooded,
her eyes on her daughter. Scaurus amused himself by throwing a
remark at her now and then. When she failed to respond, he
would pointedly repeat it to Gratidia over Helvia's head. He
managed to make Helvia appear ill-humoured and rude. But
Marcus Scaurus looked with approval on Fufidia. Charming and
modest, he thought her. Lucius might have chosen a worse
mother for his future sons.

She for whom the feast was given seemed to enjoy it least.

Fufidia was silent. Charmingly dressed in muslin, the warmth and excitement had brought to her golden skin a deeper colour. Her long blond hair shone in the lamplight. But her smiles were abstracted and fleeting. Lucius, beside her, played his part, the picture of the devoted husband-to-be, dividing his time between whispered words to Fufidia and witticisms addressed to Scaurus' wife on his other side.

"You wash your hands," he observed, as the servant poured perfumed water over the girl's hands. "But you do not eat. Let me tempt you with grapes." He held a bunch to her lips.

"Don't make me."

"Your father gives us good food. Old Bald-pate would have a fit to see us putting all this away. He'd have half of it carted off here and now."

She refused to laugh at his jibes at Caesar.

"Look at Aunt Caecilia lying there stuffing herself as though she hasn't eaten for a week. There are three dates left on the plate of the aunt next to her. I wager that she takes them. Will she? Won't she? Yes, there they go. And already she has filled her napkin with food to take home with her."

He continued to talk lightly and engagingly to Fufidia, but her eyes were more on Cinna who had just joined the party and taken his place beside her brother Quintus. They talked seriously in low tones and this set them apart, for now wine flowed and the party was animated.

A young man of the Scauri family who was on Cinna's other hand began to pump Cinna about Caesar. The young man was well fleshed and slightly bulbous of eye. It was said he was learned in the law. Curiosity now conquered his diffidence.

"I know you are friend to Caesar. Tell me one thing. You *would* say Caesar was right to receive the senators sitting in his chair that day, when they voted him those exceptional honours?" He added, "In that golden chair, I suppose it was!"

"I don't think Caesar was well that day." Cinna did not like the young man's eyes.

The fleshy face leaned closer and said, "Tell me, did you really draw up a bill legitimising Caesar's—er union with any woman he wants for . . . for," he sniggered convulsively, "the procreation of children?"

Cinna looked pityingly at him.

"As a little reason must dispose immediately of such nonsense, I assume it is the Falernian talking now!"

The other was uncomprehending.

"A rumour which began about Caesar's marriage to a certain queen has been distended to embrace the whole female sex. You may discount the lot," Cinna declared.

"Ah, just so." The young man nodded confidentially and drank once more.

"At least such stories were never concocted about a more sober man than Caesar," Cinna added bitingly. And he turned once more to his nephew.

"I am told there is to be an entertainment. Dancers, perhaps?" demanded an aunt of Lucius.

"Not dancers," Lucius returned. "A pity, but no dancers. Jugglers and then poetry."

"Poetry? I never heard of that," she said.

"You don't get around. It's the latest thing at banquets. Like lying with the men," he added, *sotto voce.*

None of the Aemilian women had done this before, and only now had the pleasures of food and wine lessened their embarrassment.

Fufidia succeeded in making her brother look at her. She gave him a tremulous smile, and was rewarded by a loving glance.

"It is arranged by my uncle Cinna," she said hurriedly to the aunt. "It is a poetry reading with actors. It is the best poem of Catullus, who was a friend of my mother and my uncle. It is a famous poem."

"Catullus. Fancy that," returned the Aemilian aunt languidly, with disinterest.

"Just as well it's Catullus," said Lucius, looking towards Cinna. "The fellow's dead and doesn't bite."

"That is a strange thing to say," returned the aunt.

"I'm in a strange mood tonight." Lucius gave a laugh. He pulled Fufidia's hair, his eyes on her perfect profile. "Where is Callirrhoe now?" he whispered. He put his cheek to hers. *"Voluptas mea,* smile for me," he breathed.

Fufidia did not respond, though she attempted a smile. Probably, Lucius thought, she was nervous. He doubted if she had ever attended a banquet before, let alone one given in her honour. He looked at her little rosy fingers as they fiddled with some nuts. The hands of a child still, suited to childish activities. He could scarcely realize how in awe she was of her father, who expected conventional happiness from her marriage, how afraid of old Marcus Scaurus—no, terrified of him and of his family *en bloc,* who would soon be her family. No doubt she was steeling herself for what would be a great effort.

Fufidia looked over again to her brother. Young Quintus was saying, with his eyes, what he had said to her in words before. "Oh Fufih. Fufidiola *mea.* I don't want this to happen. It is not right, this marriage."

He had blurted it out in a burst of anger and emotion. He had not said why. He had called Lucius a brute, a scoundrel.

With a shout and commotion, jugglers appeared. They stood in the centre. One man did wonders with a heap of little balls, another with an incredible number of plates. The first played tricks with eggs. Lucius set down his wine goblet, and got to his feet to see better. Most of the diners did the same.

Lucius soon lost interest and took out his dice-box. Deftly he threw several times onto the table before himself and Fufidia. Now he seemed extraordinarily absorbed in the dice and the girl beside him heard him curse angrily at a series of bad throws. Banging the dice-box down on the table, he swallowed half the contents of his wineglass and turned back to join the group around the jugglers.

Gratidia levered herself up painfully from her couch. "Eh, it is agony to lie so," she complained, "to lie without moving." One hand to her side, she hobbled over to Fufidia, and sat beside her for a moment to ease her back. "I think I must go to my room now."

"I will tell my mother." Fufidia slipped off the couch and mingled with the spectators for a moment.

Taking advantage of Lucius' absence, Quintus hurried over to help his aunt. Then Helvia came and insisted on taking Gratidia out herself. She then stayed away long enough for the Scauri to begin whispering at her rudeness. The jugglers had departed by the time she reappeared and Helvia almost missed the beginning of Catullus.

The story of Peleus and Thetis was offered with the cheese and fruit. Against the painted portico with its vivid skies and glistening trees, the narrator summoned up the blue salt seas and the swift pinewood ship of the Argonauts, spun in the glittering hexameters of Catullus, as Peleus fell in love, watching the sea goddess Thetis' lovely body rise from the waves. The voice of the narrator soared and sang as all Thessaly flocked to the palace for the wedding, with the glitter of gold and silver and ivory thrones, and then passed to the lament of Ariadne, standing on the wave-sounding shore to watch Theseus sail off with swift fleet, wild sadness in her heart. Theseus lashed the waters with his oars, leaving to the raging gale his empty vows to love her.

Ariadne had a sweet musical voice, and the Aemilian ladies might have wept, if they had not eaten so much. But wine flowed and brought a little quickening appreciation of Ariadne's pitiful cry:

"Not these the promises you once gave me
With smooth and winning voice. Ah no!
To this poor wretch you gave the hope of happy marriage,
Longed-for union, which now all the winds of Heaven Scatter null and void."

The ladies nodded and smiled as the story of heartbreak rang in their ears. Marcus Scaurus chewed grapes and enjoyed the wine.

"It's only that the feller's so long-winded," he muttered.

Helvia heard him with contempt. She gazed at her lovely daughter—mimed, in Ariadne's complaint, as surely as the handsome young man beside her was mimed in the faithless Theseus.

Cinna perambulated, head down, appreciating again the familiar words. He stopped by Fufidia, sat down a moment, and whispering, brought a smile to her face. He saluted Lucius by a very correct inclination of the head.

The ladies, shifting thankfully to a sitting position, whispered among themselves. The poem was very long and heavy, wasn't it? Very heavy and monotonous? A little knot of ladies talked stealthily about anything but the poem.

The fleshy-faced Aemilian cousin had got to his feet and came to Lucius, leaning over him. His perfume mingled with the sweat his drinking had worked up. His little beard wagged in time with his words as he said, "We're sitting ducks . . . agony, isn't it? I'd lie down and snore if I didn't keep walking."

Lucius gaped at him. Unaccountably and suddenly, as he watched his cousin's face, that face was becoming lop-sided, like a piece of pastry lightly kneaded. Lucius' eyes rolled. The whole scene had taken on the lurid images and disproportion of drunkenness. Beside him his aunt's face leered oddly and he heard voices through a wall of water. He saw flickering darts of light. He knew his father was watching him. He also knew that he was not drunk. His father's gaze kept him from slumping. But for the very life of him he could not hold his head straight and it ached horribly. His limbs hurt. And he breathed hard. He was just aware of young Quintus Fufidius' face, the eyes burning into him, just as on that other night at Eucharis'.

The actors had finished. Marcus Scaurus gave the signal for departure. Lucius had not seemed to be drinking too much, but suddenly he was showing all the signs of it. A cousin helped hoist Lucius to his feet. The whole group of the Aemilii Scauri went into the long recital of thanks and farewell. Lucius was borne away amongst them.

As he said goodbye, Scaurus commented on the uniqueness of the dinner party. He could remember no other dinner where almost two hours were spent on improving the minds of the guests with poetry. Helvia replied that she had not intended to undertake so formidable a task as that. Of course, dancing girls might have been better.

XVI

Going home, Marcus Scaurus was in high good humour. His son had annoyed him by slumping at the end of the evening, but probably no one had noticed it. No doubt he would grow out of this sort of indulgence. But Lucius was in another carriage and Scaurus was free to ponder on the Fufidii. The standard of entertainment had been high. The Fufidii were a presentable family in their wealth—evident in the house and its appointments. No suggestion there of the display or of the grossness of manners which so branded some of these farmers and businessmen when they got money. Good-looking too . . .

"It was done well tonight," he remarked with satisfaction to his wife. "I have made a sensible contract there. What do you say?"

He was not in the least interested in what she would say, but he threw her a word now and then.

She sighed. "I think," said Papiria, in her long-suffering fashion, "that the wife of Quintus Fufidius is *mal'educata.*"

"H'm. Well . . ."

"She won't look at you," pursued Papiria.

"She is good to look at, though. Like her daughter. Lots of hair—very fine hair: blond, too."

"I suppose she thought it a good occasion to show off with poetry," said Papiria, quite snappily for her.

Scaurus yawned.

"I thought you liked things of the mind."

"Of course, she knows it is a very good marriage for her daughter. You can see how the daughter adores Lucius. She follows him with her eyes."

"Does she? I didn't notice much of that tonight. Kept her eyes down. But there—they're the prettiest eyes you could wish for."

His wife sighed.

"I would ask you, *coniunx carissima*, what is there to sigh about!" he demanded in exasperation.

She said nothing. Scaurus wished he still had Mucia and that she had not left him for Pompeius. He had been fond of Mucia. She didn't wilt and she didn't sigh. She had spirit. And she was the mother of his sons. A womanly woman, Mucia. For a little while he pondered, pleasantly, on just what he meant by that.

In the blaze of torchlight, the carriages rattled and thundered over the stone of the Argiletum and down the Via Sacra under one of Rome's winter nights of starlit radiance from a frost-glittering sky. On the high podium of the temple of Castor and Pollux, the two youths on their white horses gleamed with brave promise. "We are your saviours, Romans," the Dioscuri said. "We await now the army of your knights parading before us, glorious with banners." Ghosts peopled the sleeping black darkness as the carriage rounded the tall brick temple with its high portico and the marble splendour of its columns before slowing and turning under the round massive brick arches of the Via Nova, between the House of the Vestal Virgins and Vesta's sacred grove. They passed close to Scaurus' old house, the scene of past splendours, then finally climbed the Caelian Hill.

At home, Marcus Scaurus stood in the atrium of his present, comparatively modest house among the oak trees, and as was his wont, rapped with his stick until his personal slaves showed up.

"All right. Get me to bed," he said curtly. To his wife, who stood there as if for dismissal, he added, "There, you may leave off those expectant looks, my dear. I shan't need you tonight."

He chuckled at her expression. What a good lugubrious idiot the woman was. Her money was run through long since, but it had saved him in a difficult situation.

"Where's Lucius?" he asked, as an afterthought.

"Already in bed, master," Lucius' man announced. "He is already sleeping."

Scaurus had thought it best that his son should sleep in the family home that night.

The young Aemilian cousin appeared and said to Scaurus, "Lucius breathes so heavily. I think he is ill."

"I doubt it," returned Scaurus. "I'll look at him."

His face softened at the sight of Lucius, sprawled elegantly on his bed, one arm flung high above his head. He might snore very loudly but he was as handsome as any young man could wish to be. His father said gruffly, "He's perfectly all right. Turn him over."

The slave turned the boy over and Lucius stopped snoring.

"He does breathe oddly," insisted the cousin.

"He'll sleep it off. Bit too much wine, that's all." Scaurus did not like the cousin to see his son drunk.

"I'll be in the next room," said the young cousin, who was staying the night with them. "I'll look in on Lucius after a while. One can't trust slaves."

But the cousin did not wake. In the early hours of the morning it was Lucius' own slave who crept in with a lamp. But by then the stertorous breathing had stopped altogether. Lucius was sunk in sleep now. But it was that sleep from which no one wakes.

At dawn, Marcus Scaurus was woken by his head slave, whose face showed such urgency that Scaurus struggled up.

"Domine . . ." The man's voice was husky with fear. "The young master . . . come quickly."

"What's that? What . . ."

"Master!" The man wrung his hands. "Master, he is dead. Dead, dead in his sleep."

Was he still dreaming, Scaurus wondered. But the flickering lamp, the ghastly face of the man, the cold marble dolphins on the black and white of the floor underfoot, the pale oblong of the dawn sky from the half-shuttered window—these were reality. Dragging his bad foot, he lumbered after the slave.

Lucius was lying twisted on his bed, with half-closed eyes, one open palm upturned as though he had sought help at the end— help not forthcoming.

"Get the doctor quickly. Get Mucia—she knows where to find him. Not Mucia, you fool—I mean Papiria. She knows."

"I have already summoned the doctor, *Domine.*" The slave trembled with fright.

Scaurus knelt down and felt the boy's pulse, put his head down to the boy's heart. Then hard long-drawn sobs shook him. He sat up on the bed and cradled Lucius' head in his arms, groaning with horror. Finally he set him down and shouted like a madman for the doctor . . . for anyone, for some reason for his boy to . . . oh, but it could not be . . .

Without in the least achieving anything, there was a frightful running to and fro of slaves. The doctor came, a clever old Greek who had attended the family for years. He examined Lucius carefully and shook his head.

"There is nothing to be done for him now," he said to Marcus Scaurus. "I fear poison."

In mid-morning, in his house, Fufidius stared hard at the sharp face of the Lydian who had been conducted before him. The Lydian was one of Marcus Scaurus' slaves and he had brought the startling story that Lucius Scaurus had been found dead that morning, dead in his bed. The doctor said it was poison.

"Who sent you here?"

"No one, *Domine.*"

Fufidius' head was reeling. "Send him off."

Scaurus' man turned and then looked back meaningfully.

"You can give him some money," Fufidius told his own slave. He hardly knew he said the words. He was stunned. There was no reason for the Lydian to lie. Lucius Scaurus dead. Dead after a banquet in the Fufidii home. Fufidius sat down heavily, trying to believe it. The gods played with him, played with them all. All this effort, all the talk, the arranging, the money, Fufidia's happiness, Helvia's . . . Helvia's hatred of the boy. The Scauri were still powerful. What if the death were put at Fufidius' door? Poisoned, the man had said.

Fufidius called Helvia to him. Burdened with the dreadful news, he hardly noticed her black-shadowed eyes, her trembling lips.

"I am told Lucius Scaurus is dead. He has been poisoned."

The effect on Helvia was shocking. He was not prepared for the relief that flooded her face, for her muttered, "Thanks be to the gods." Almost she babbled in her eagerness for details.

"Helvia!" he cried. "What has happened to you? Have you no feeling? Your daughter's fiancé is dead."

"What?" Helvia was still busy digesting the news, standing silently, her expression serene now.

"Helvia! What have you done?" He stood in front of her, forcing her wandering gaze to meet his.

"I? Done? Done what?"

"You know what I found in the tree!" He looked round to make sure they were alone. "You know quite well what I mean. I found the evidence of your—experiments. Your intimacy with the occult. What I could never have believed of you if I had not seen the thing with my own eyes . . ."

She did not answer him. "I must send word to my brother," she muttered, and made as if to turn and go.

"Helvia! Are you mad? Your behaviour is incomprehensible! I know—and others too by now, because servants will have talked—that you've used spells and charms and the gods know what else. You have made your dislike of Lucius Scaurus publicly evident on every occasion you have met him. Now he is dead. Poisoned, they say. After eating and drinking at our home!"

She shrugged. "You tell me that it is so. What would you have me do?"

"At least stop smiling—the first time you have smiled, I believe, since I made the contract of marriage! At least hide your pleasure. If he has really been poisoned, do you imagine it will rest at that?" Fufidius flung himself down on a seat and buried his face in his hands. "May the immortal gods save us now!"

Helvia looked squarely at him then, for the first time. Her face softened. She went over to him and spoke gently. "I believe the immortal gods are indeed saving us, saving Fufidia. Do not give way. It is true I did not want this marriage. You know it well enough. I have acted for the best. Fufa is a child. I could not bear her to marry Lucius Scaurus."

Fufidius gazed at her without speaking. His face was very grave. And still apprehensive.

"But I must get word to Gaius," Helvia said urgently.

"You can tell your brother," he said, in a tired way.

Helvia went out and he was alone.

He noted that Cinna had to be told straightaway. But she had not thought to tell the one person who should first be told—Fufidia.

Before he told his daughter, however, Fufidius sent his own freedman to the house of the Scauri, to make quite certain of what had happened. The man returned with nothing further to tell. But there was no mistake.

Perhaps tragedy already hung in the air, perhaps it had seeped in through the pores of her skin. Fufidia was hardly surprised when the news was broken to her. They tried to do it gently. She cut through her parents' words almost brutally. "He is dead, isn't he, Papa?"

"It is so, *filiola*. He has died at the hand of another. It was not a natural death."

"Did he suffer, Papa?"

"No. He was unconscious for the last hours."

"He was ill at the dinner last night."

"Probably. And we all thought he had simply drunk too much."

"He did not drink much," said the little girl quietly. Suddenly she turned on her heel and fled from the room.

Helvia ran after her. But Fufidia lay on her bed, her hands over her ears. She would not listen to anyone, not even her mother. She begged to be left alone.

"Of course, he was already ill," was Gratidia's simple reaction.

She remained in bed that day. She was old, she said, too old for such calamities. She shut herself up with her serving women, while the household reverberated with the shock.

"So he's dead," was all Quintus had to say to the news. He looked intently at his father, his eyes gleaming.

"I would have thought it a matter of some regret," returned Fufidius bitterly.

"Regret!" Quintus walked away head down, then turned to confront his father. "Uncle Cinna knew what he was like. How can I regret such a lucky escape for Fufidia, Papa," he burst out. "An escape from a man as rotten inside as—as he was fair outside."

"Rotten inside . . ." repeated Fufidius slowly.

"You can't say anything else, Papa," vowed the boy passionately. "Uncle Gaius got him off nicely—"

"What do you mean 'got him off?' "

Quintus drew back, but his father forced him to go on. "Oh, a poem he wrote about Lucius," he muttered reluctantly. One day a friend of his had said something to him about a poem—and then hastily retracted.

"When was this?" Fufidius forced him to go on.

"Uncle Gaius' poem was read out at the poetry meeting at Eucharis' during the Saturnalia."

"On Lucius."

"Yes."

"What was in that poem?" demanded Fufidius.

His son hesitated.

"You said it 'got him off!' "

"About him deserting from the battle of Thapsus," mumbled Quintus.

"Don't you conceal anything from me!" ordered his father sternly.

"It said his highest talent was sexual submission to another man," the boy said jerkily. "It was a brilliant poem."

"What else didn't I know about my own future son-in-law?" asked Fufidius bitterly of Cinna when a hurried note brought him round later that day.

"You're well rid of him." Cinna brought a healthier air into the stricken house, the air of the outside world. He had come straight from the Senate House and was formally dressed. Fufidius was hardly ever home at this hour of the morning and so there was a feeling of unreality about their meeting.

"How could you deliberately have had that poem read in public?"

Fufidius was very angry indeed.

Dramatically, the two stood in confrontation. The complicated folds of his toga enhanced Cinna's height. He was rather hot and sweaty from his energetic morning and his head was thrown back in slightly arrogant fashion, his keen blue eyes intent. Fufidius was only slightly less tall and more strongly built. Anxiety had darkened his face.

"I wanted to stop him marrying Fufidia. I wanted to provoke

him into attacking me. He was too drunk." Cinna watched the effect of his words.

"Oh, I understand you. Of course, the most reasonable thing in the world, wasn't it? And honourable too! You couldn't have addressed your objections to me!"

"You would not have listened, though. You wouldn't listen to Helvia."

"What right had you to step in?" Fufidius half shouted, half wept.

"What right? I am fond of Fufidia."

"By Hercules! She is *my* daughter and I had arranged this for her! Now the boy has been poisoned after dining here . . ."

Helvia came in and the two men turned to her. "Oh, she suffers, my child, how she suffers." Helvia's hand went up to her mouth and she bit on her clenched fingers. "Perhaps he should have been left to live . . ."

"Helvia!" Fufidius said desperately. "What are you saying? Did you . . ." He could not utter the words.

"I mean the gods might have had him die later, in war," she returned slowly, almost reflectively. Her eyes met his absently. "It would not have been so dreadful for Fufidia."

"Oh, but he would have run away, wouldn't he?" Fufidius shouted angrily at her. "He ran away from battles! Your brother has celebrated it in verse!" He looked at them standing there. He was isolated in his own family and afraid.

Fufidia stayed by herself in her own room. It was Chaereas she mourned. Chaereas, who had been the ideal lover, who had appeared as Lucius, whom she had adored, whom she had believed in—against her mother, her uncle, her brother, even against what she had overheard with her own ears. Lucius had proved wicked. But how she had loved.

XVII

To the outside world Marcus Scaurus might preserve a stoic fortitude. In the depths of the family home his grief and rage confounded all. His life, he thought, was diminished now by half. There were no grandchildren; one son was dead, and his only other defeated and on the run in Spain. Lucius had brought down his father's wrath often enough, but to a point he had been amenable. He had fought in Greece and he had fought in Africa. His money might have run like water, but he had dutifully sought—and found—a rich girl to marry. He had not been the first young noble to live to the limit. His beauty had drawn many to him—men and women. Could he be blamed for this power of attraction? When he cared to, Lucius had charmed his father as well.

Then, poisoned. Poisoned on the verge of restoring the family fortunes. Cruel, incredible, unbearable. Lucius Aemilius Scaurus, of old patrician stock, poisoned like a dog. Close on Marcus Scaurus' grief there followed deep anger. Despite his bad foot, he could not rest and walked the floor for hours—and vowed vengeance.

His mystification was almost as great as his anger. The hastily called family conference revealed nothing. The doctor had named a poison—aconite. A poison not detectable in wine or food. Lucius had been among friends and family. Impossible to think of anyone present killing him. One of Lucius' sexual partners, someone who had a grudge against him and who had bribed a slave? What slave? One of Lucius' own servants had accompanied him to the banquet, one of a mere handful who looked after the rather lowly attic his son had lived in for the past months in Rome, in the Subura. The man was a Lydian. Scaurus shouted for him. But, said someone, he had returned to the apartment of his master after Lucius had gone to bed.

"Send for all his servants and get them here quickly," Scaurus ordered his freedman.

"Would you allow me to question them on your behalf, *Domine?*" asked the man, trembling at his master's face.

"Get them here. They'll talk here—and if they're concealing anything, by all the gods, I'll crucify them!"

And Scaurus meant no more nor less than what he said.

But questioning the slaves had to be forgone—or postponed. By the time Scaurus' freedman got there, Lucius' slaves had disappeared. Prudently—in certain anticipation of torture.

The formalities of death required attention. Undertakers had been engaged. The death had been registered at the temple of Libitina. Lucius lay on a bed of ivory in the atrium of his father's house, his feet towards the door. The house was draped in black, with branches of cypress outside the door. Among the letters of condolence was a long epistle from Quintus Fufidius. It spoke of his sorrow in language so splendid it might have come from Cicero. Close on the letter came a deputation from the Fufidii requesting to pay their respects to the dead.

Scaurus had spent some time by now with Quintus Fufidius. He had developed a condescending regard and respect for him. The death of Lucius changed everything. Now the family in whose house his son had come to grief was hateful to him. However, the Fufidii were received—received by a solid block of Scaurus' relatives, with Scaurus at their head. Scaurus was of grim countenance indeed, his face softening only at the sight of the little Fufidia. But his manner was cold to Helvia and Quintus, and he made it clear without words that the death had raised an insurmountable barrier between the clans.

Lucius lay in state for seven days, after which the beautiful boy, who in life had aroused such adoration in some, such hatred in others, was taken out with all possible honours. The funeral cortège was not the most magnificent of its kind, but it was impressive enough, with lighted torches, a flautist and women mourners who tore their hair as they sang dirges. Dead ancestors came, too—masked souls who were carried behind in chariots, Consul Aemilius Scaurus, Lucius' grandfather, among them. Living relatives followed, the men veiled, the women dishevelled of

hair. There was a *laudatio* in the Forum, the oration given by
Marcus Valerius Messalla, who said less of Lucius than of the
boy's famous forebears, who sat in a row on chairs, their wax
masks eerily realistic.

Then Lucius was carried to his funeral pyre outside the city
walls, wrapped in a shroud of amianthus and sprinkled with perfume. Turning his head away, Scaurus set light to the pine
branches with a torch. When the flames had consumed the body,
they were extinguished with wine. Scaurus gathered the bones
and placed them in an urn with roses and aromatic plants. The
urn was then taken to its resting place in the family tomb on the
Via Appia.

To the feast offered for relatives and friends of the dead man
on the following day, the Fufidii were most conspicuously not
invited.

The purification of the house was scarcely over, the floor cere-
monially swept with branches of verbena, when Lucius' creditors
began to assail his father. Scaurus had gloomy words with his
secretary/freedman, also with the bulbous-eyed Aemilius
Scaurus, who was learned in the law.

Scaurus was in sore straits.

"I've a certain amount coming to me on paper, but will my
debtors ever pay me all they owe?" he asked dismally. "And
many are old sums, too, owed by men out of the country—dead
or in exile. And I've debts enough of my own now, without
Lucius'."

The cousin's eyes became ever more bulbous as requests
poured in. In all, Lucius had owed well over half a million *sestertii,* including debts incurred by him on the surety of that marriage which had never come about.

Long confabulations with the cousin pushed the unhappy man
to the limit. Not noted for his good temper, Scaurus was near to
hating Decimus Scaurus for his eyes, for his excellent advice.
Scaurus sent him away.

Then, in the midst of all these problems, a message reached
him from Eucharis, asking urgently if she might see him. She had
information of great importance. Scaurus did not think anything
she might have to tell him could be very important, but he sent
word he would go to her place that evening.

XVIII

The Marcus Scaurus who arrived was depressed and harsh, his strong face drawn by the tragedy. Eucharis set herself to ease his misery as much as she could, bringing him the choicest of her wine, serving him in that special way she had. When he had washed his hands, when wine had blunted the edge of his suffering, she said, standing before him, her eyes brilliant with invention, "You must be concerned to know who murdered your son."

She had his full attention as she continued. "There is something you should know . . . Helvia hated him."

Scaurus stared hard at her. "Well?"

"She was always opposed to the marriage."

"This is hardly news to me," he said scornfully.

"She is a bad woman," said Eucharis very quietly.

Scaurus looked at her impatiently. All very well for the little Eucharis to indulge in backbiting. But what did it have to do with Lucius' death?

"Helvia is guilty of two crimes."

"Are you telling me she killed my son?"

She hesitated, then plunged. "She has made spells."

"What!"

"She has named Lucius in a spell." And Eucharis told Scaurus what she had learned from the friendly slave of the Fufidii.

Scaurus' face darkened.

"It is obvious," pursued Eucharis delicately, "why she wanted the help of magic spells."

Scaurus felt fury rise in him as he digested the information, his mind working quickly. Could he believe Eucharis? Yes, it made sense! Helvia. Ah, he would make her suffer for what she had done, for his grief and fury. His belief in her guilt was immediate and absolute. She it was who had administered the poison.

"What about the other crime?"

Eucharis looked at him intently. "Listen to me very carefully, please. For very many years the *Domina* and her brother Cinna have been lovers."

Scaurus started. "You know this?"

"I have proof."

"What proof?"

"For many years I have kept a poem, a letter-poem, which I . . . found . . ."

"Stole, yes, go on . . ."

"Stole," agreed Eucharis, "when I was a young slave of the *Domina*. In Arpinum. She treated me very badly. I was the nurse of her children. She hated me. I have never understood why."

"It could not be on account of her husband's relationship with you, of course!"

Eucharis cast down her eyes. "Women can be cruel to other women," she said. "I was a good nurse to her children and she repaid me with unkindness—nothing but unkindness." Eucharis' lips trembled and tears welled. "Finally she sent me away. You know this. I took this letter with me. It is in verse. I kept it in case the *Domina* might try to harm me." Eucharis breathed quickly. "If you will promise me that you will not tell anyone where you got it, I shall give you the poem. There is one thing I would ask . . ."

"Let me see this poem."

Eucharis produced a little roll of paper and handed it to him. When he had read it, Scaurus said, "You have done well." His eyes were alive now. "What is the other thing you said? You've got some other request."

She looked a little flustered and then spoke rather quickly. "If Helvia is accused—er, if you accuse her, and she is found guilty, I want to have the opportunity of buying—er, very cheaply, from you—one of her forfeited estates. The one at Lavinium."

Despite himself Scaurus almost laughed. She was a quick little schemer. Beautiful and clever too.

"You could arrange it," she added.

"Yes, I could arrange it—if I won the case. By all the gods, Eucharis, your mind works well enough."

"All I have told you is true."

"Yes."

She insisted, gently, now. "Shall we say four hundred thousand *sestertii?* No more than four hundred thousand as the price of the property?"

"Very well."

"We have made a contract?"

Scaurus did laugh then, even if mirthlessly. "We have made a contract," he agreed.

Eucharis sat motionless for a long time after Scaurus left, her heart throbbing as waves of excitement, of joy, of fear ran through her. Shades rose from the past. She relived that day when Helvia had coldly ordered her to abort. She saw the doctor coming with the loathsome instruments of his craft . . . now, on her knees, she was pleading with Helvia, could feel Helvia's cruel fingers now, digging into her as she dragged her towards him. At the sight of a long bronze needle Eucharis had gone mad, had fought and struggled. The doctor, a weakly man, had hastily suggested to Helvia that Eucharis take drugs instead. But Eucharis had fought this too.

Again she heard Helvia storm to Gratidia, "Ecastor! Anyone would think we were trying to murder her!"

And Gratidia's indifferent aside, "It's often one way to do it."

What had passed between them? Eucharis didn't know, but in the end she was allowed to bear Pamphilus. Only to have Helvia order him to be killed by exposure. *Her* baby to be killed, when at least twenty or so children had been born to slaves of the family and reared within it.

Of course, both mistress and slave knew perfectly well why, though no word of it was ever spoken.

Probably at Gratidia's insistence, Eucharis was finally allowed to keep Pamphilus on condition she went to the wife of Titus Fadius, who wanted a nurse for her new baby. So Eucharis had been taken down to Rome, and Pamphilus as well.

Eucharis' fingers shook slightly as she poured herself a little wine and water and swallowed it. But her brain worked coolly enough now. She could become a wealthy woman—if Helvia were only accused and found guilty. In this case little Pamphilus could be well provided for. If Helvia were acquitted, Fufidius would know nothing of her role and she could hope to keep him. She would of course like to keep Fufidius. But, sadly, she had finally realised that Fufidius would never be wholly generous to her, would never adopt their son as long as her enemy Helvia was head of his household in Rome.

When he got home, Scaurus said to his freedman, "Where is Decimus?"

"You told me to send him off, *Domine.*"

"Well, get him back."

Bore though Decimus Scaurus was, he was well versed in the law.

XIX

The summons was served by three men from the office of the
Praetor Urbanus M. Junius Brutus. They were brusque and peremptory, exuding petty officialdom and the power of the law.
They gave the written document to Fufidius because they had no
experience of serving a summons on a woman of Helvia's class.
Only women of the lower classes appeared in court—not sheltered, rich women.

Standing in the middle of his atrium, Fufidius read the single
sheet, noting even that the scribe had got Helvia's childhood
domicile wrong. Helvia accused! His mind cried out in terror.
He went on standing there, while the noises of early morning
sounded in the background. He heard Helvia's voice as she
talked to the head serving woman, explaining something about
some dresses that she wanted cleaned. Then he knew she had
come into the atrium, because of the sudden intensity of the
men's eyes as they looked past him.

Helvia's presence was required before the Praetor Lucius
Marcius Philippus three days hence when M. Aemilius Scaurus
would formally denounce her. *Criminis delatio.* A criminal
charge. The crime alleged was murder of his son. The Praetor
would decide if there was evidence enough to proceed. Fufidius
had no option but to sign. Helvia should have signed, but the
men accepted her husband's signature. Probably they thought
she could not write. And they had looked their fill and wanted to
get away.

Fufidius stayed holding the copy they had left him, his eyes
travelling again and again over the grim phrases. He heard his
wife's voice behind him. Very slowly he turned, afraid to break
the news, trying to find words. She snatched the writ and
smoothed the papyrus sheet out. Her head bent over it for an
interminable time. All Fufidius' antagonism to her was gone

now. He wanted only to save her from this awful blow, which was going to shatter and lay waste all their lives.

Helvia raised her head. Her face was crumpled. She put her hands out, asking for help. He took her arms and helped her to a chair. Her lips trembled as she tried to absorb it. "I am to be accused of murder." Her voice was strangely muffled. "I am to be *rea.*"

"Not at this stage. It is an interrogation only."

"I must be present?"

"Can you not face it?"

She covered her face with her hands. Then she looked up. "Can they try me in my absence?"

"Of course not. Nor do I think they can condemn you in your absence. But you could not remain in Italy." He looked at her and said, his own voice trembling, "Perhaps I can send you away . . . Greece. I have connections enough." It sounded unreal to him even as he said it.

She shook her head hopelessly.

"Helvia!" he said urgently. "I will do everything I can. We have money. Much can be done with money. If you stand trial, you will have the best defence I can find."

He put his arms round her. She felt soft and yielding. He had forgotten the feel of her in all these years. She had seemed unapproachable with her firm-fleshed statuesque body. Whatever she had done, he wanted to save her. For all their sakes.

On the morning of a dark, stormy day of late January, Marcus Scaurus made his way to the office of the Praetor M. Calpurnius Piso, who was in charge of the standing criminal court which inquired into cases of poisoning. Some days before, he had gone before the Praetor L. Marcius Philippus, a man well known to him, and had requested formal permission to charge Helvia and sworn an oath that he had adequate grounds.

Two of his own men forced a way for him now through the crowd of pushing, litigious humanity in the precincts of the Basilica Julia. A white-faced Helvia, supported by her husband, was already there. The praetor's office was divided by curtains from the rest of the hall, and in front of Piso, Scaurus made certain assertions concerning the character of the accused. His eyes raked Helvia pitilessly as he spoke. She had, he said, always opposed the marriage of her daughter with his son. He would produce evidence as well of magic practices and of incest.

A tight band seemed to constrict Helvia's head. She stood there and listened to the cruel words and felt the curious, hard eyes of the Praetor wander over her as he put questions to Scaurus.

There was the scratch of the secretary's pen on the papyrus sheet, the rapid shorthand of a scribe on a wax tablet.

"The woman is wealthy in her own right. . . . It is submitted that she did not wish her wealth to pass to a young man not of her choice . . .

"Yes, the banquet had been on the Nones of January; yes, lasting from the third hour until the sixth hour of the night. They had been a large party. Opportunity there was . . ."

"And your assertion is that the woman put poison in food or wine?"

"It is so."

The Praetor then turned his attention to Helvia. "Did you put poison in food or wine?"

"No."

"You could have?"

Helvia forced her head high. Her hands expressed—with artistry—her assent, combined with distaste for the mere suggestion.

"There were almost thirty diners in the dining room. All had equal opportunity."

"You are to answer simply yes or no to the question."

"Yes, I had opportunity."

Helvia had gathered all her forces for this interview, but a pulse beat in her throat and made it hard to talk.

"You are making a confession of guilt?" The Praetor's eyes were cold.

"I am *not*. I am innocent of the charges."

There was a pause, then the Praetor began talking in a monotonous drone. The scribes wrote hard.

"I am satisfied that there should be a trial. In addition to murder, the woman is accused of several offences—of poisoning and magic practices, and . . ." he paused, "of incest."

There had been no mistake. She had heard aright the first time the word was uttered. Incest. Now she was stunned with horror. Cold fingers laid hold of her heart. The closely guarded secret of years . . . impossible that the Praetor should know, that anyone should know . . . She hardly heard the rest . . .

". . . for the purposes of the trial, the charges are narrowed down to the most important, which in this case is murder by poisoning."

The Praetor drew up an inscription, which was passed to the judge in charge of the standing murder court. The inscription read:

Consulibus Julio Cesare et Marco Antonio VII KAL. FEB. Apud Praetorem M. Calpurnium Pisonem, M. Aemilius Scaurus professus est se Helviam lege Cornelia de veneficiis ream deferre quod dicat eam, Non. Jan., domo suo consulibus illis veneno necasse Lucium filium.

(the 26th day of January, before the Praetor M. Calpurnius Piso, M. Aemilius Scaurus has formally declared that he charges Helvia under the *lex Cornelia de veneficiis* of having, in her own house, on the 5th January in the year of their consulship, poisoned his son.)

The charge was admitted by the *Iudex.* The president of the court then fixed a day for her trial before the full court, on the 25th of February, or V KAL. MART., one month hence.

The best defence money can buy—Gratidia, ailing and dishevelled but concentrating all her will, sought Fufidius out. She sat huddled on a sofa, her old eyes staring from a ravaged face.

"We must get Cicero."

Fufidius had hardly dared to think of Cicero, and said so.

"We are related," rasped Gratidia. "His grandfather married a Gratidia."

"But Cicero's life is remote from ours."

"Like us, he is from Arpinum."

"If he pleads nowadays, it is before Caesar, in Caesar's house," said Fufidius. "On behalf of a king, for instance," he added. He meant King Deiotarus.

"He has defended private people in the past. This will not be a political trial, but he might oblige us."

"We will try."

"Get him," said the old woman. "Get him. He will save Helvia. Hardly ever has Cicero lost a case. I will speak to him myself. You will arrange it. We will write a letter first."

Fufidius considered. "The Aemilii will put up a persuasive case," he said slowly. "They have the connections . . . but," fear made his face ugly, "but I have the money."

"Helvia's property," Gratidia demanded suddenly. "If she were convicted . . ."

"It would be confiscated," he returned grimly.

"All that wealth!"

"All that wealth. Yes."

Forthwith they set to compose the letter, which was carried by Fufidius' headman for delivery into Cicero's own hands. There was no time to be lost. The situation was as grave as it could be. Though they had known Lucius' death could bring great trouble to them, Scaurus' accusation of Helvia was worse than anything they had thought of.

Fufidius found some relief, now, in action, even if it was only to call in loans and to realise on some property. He felt fully master in his own house once more, that they all looked to him for direction.

Things moved fast. The very day after receiving their letter, Cicero called Fufidius and Helvia to him. On arrival they were led straight in. Cicero brushed aside the clients who had engaged his attention.

Immediately he declared that he would defend Helvia. But the charge was serious. Helvia would be tried for murder. As for the other two allegations, for which she was not formally on trial, incest and magic, she might expect a cruel mauling by advocates seeking to destroy her reputation. Now, was she guilty? Cicero would very much like to know. No? Then his task was the easier. He presumed that the other two allegations were—

"False. Vicious slander," declared Fufidius firmly, while his heart quaked.

Keen dark eyes searched his, searched Helvia's. They gazed back at a man still handsome, a little fleshier now in the face perhaps, but with plenty of dark hair still that waved back from a generous breadth of forehead, from finely modelled features with a good long straight nose. They could see he was master, watching that powerful intelligence assembling facts and manipulating them, coaxing or provoking from them the information which he wanted.

The death had occurred after the banquet. The hosts had to be suspect. Why had Scaurus picked on Helvia? Because of her antipathy to the son . . . yes . . . Her reason?

Who, by the way, did poison Lucius Scaurus? Did they know? No? A pity. Had the accusers any evidence but that of opportunity? It seemed not. The poison, was it known? No? Then Cicero would have inquiries made. They moved round freely during the dinner? Jugglers had entertained them? Ah, excellent opportunity, of course, for doctoring a drink. All eyes would have been trained on the jugglers.

Cicero drew Helvia out on Lucius Scaurus. Reserved at first, her hatred of him and her fears for her daughter were wrung out of her. She thought she saw understanding in his eyes. She remembered his own daughter, dead one year since, after a disastrous marriage.

She faltered often in her replies. A certain fortitude she had that all shared in an age when life was uncertain, death striking quickly and often—and sometimes early. But this lightning reversal of fortune was hard.

Cicero rose at last. There was much to do. They would need testimonials to character. Witnesses to character were no longer allowed to give evidence in person, but testimonials might be read out in court. Not without protest would the people of Arpinum see Helvia on trial, the wife of so prominent a citizen, who had done so much for their town.

Their hearts warmed. Cicero injected strength into them. There was something in what Gratidia said. This was a time when their common background told. Arpinates they were all, of that sturdy class from the *municipia,* which, the closer it advanced socially in dealings with the *optimates,* drew the more their inherent dislike. Fufidius knew he was sneered at for what was thought his presumption in having a summer villa in Tusculum, for his cascades and his fine mosaics. He suspected that

Cicero—even Cicero, who had been Consul and thereby enno-
bled, and who stood head and shoulders above them all—was
not fully at ease with the nobles. They had let him into their
closed circle in order to use his services for their infighting, but
their appreciation was always half-grudging.

Perhaps in Helvia Cicero had a case which touched his
Arpinate roots. He would put his talents to work for Helvia,
who faced such a devastating attack from this patrician over the
dead body of his son.

Not only that. The very gravity of Helvia's situation was a
challenge. It was not a case to be won or lost on evidence. For
Cicero it would be not so much to prove or disprove as to per-
suade, to weave a case of such plausibility that its rejection by the
judges would be seen as nothing but a self-imposed label of
stupidity.

In the troubled house, Fufidia was a pathetic little figure. She
prayed to her family god Lar and could be seen at times clasping
one of the dolls she had no longer to renounce. With her sweet
docility, her flower-like beauty, Fufidia had been made for laughter. Now that tragedy had struck, her life was in arrest.

One evening Fufidius heard her voice raised in passion.

"You couldn't tell me, but I knew!" Then, a faltering admission: "I heard what you said of course . . . I listened." A
pause, then, "He was wicked, wicked. . . ."

"Yes, wicked." The other voice was her brother's.

"Mamma." Fufidia's voice broke on the word. "O Quintus,
she will not . . . not . . . O Quintus! *What will happen?*"

The father heard his son's caressing voice. *"Mi mellite, mi mellite . . ."*

"O Quintus!" On a note of hopeless misery. "I can't stand it.
Mamma begged me not to marry him. I wouldn't listen."

Fufidius entered the room to see Quintus trying to calm his
sobbing, shrieking sister. She clung to him, her head buried in
his chest. At the same moment Gratidia came through another
door.

"Hysteria!" she grunted, before Fufidius had a chance to
speak. She put a hand on the girl's back and half turning, rapped
out words to a slave who had followed her in. "Get me the

fourth bottle from the end of my shelf and bring a cup." While she waited, she patted Fufidia, but the girl stayed clinging to her brother.

The slave came back and gave a bottle to the old woman.

"That's the wrong bottle," rasped Gratidia.

The slave demurred, respectfully. "It is the fourth bottle."

Gratidia went herself to check. She reappeared immediately with another bottle. She measured out a little powder into the cup, smelt it, tasted it, and made Fufidia swallow it. Quintus carried his sister to her room.

Fufidius had played no part in this scene. He watched Gratidia subside on a couch. She sat huddled in thought.

"What's the matter?" demanded Fufidius.

She raised her eyes slowly towards him without speaking.

Something struck him. "One of those bottles on your shelf must have disappeared," he said slowly. "That's why the slave brought the wrong one now."

Gratidia still said nothing, sitting there clasping cup and bottle in her hands.

"Well?"

"It got broken," she returned, without expression.

"What was in it?" asked Fufidius urgently.

All the family knew of Gratidia's drug, which was to help her out of her misery if rheumatism made life intolerable. But now Gratidia had retreated into herself. She shook her head. "It was for the gout." She would not say more.

"It *wasn't* the one for the gout, was it?" His words tore at him.

For answer, Gratidia rose and limped from the room.

XX

One of Cicero's clerks had located the doctor who had attended Lucius Scaurus. Fufidius' money coaxed a good deal of information out of him. They learned that Lucius had consulted him a few days before the banquet. Lucius had felt unwell, though he complained only of a general malaise and feeling of heaviness. When next he saw him, Lucius was dead. There was no doubt at all that he had been poisoned.

This Greek doctor was one of the cleverest in Rome. He discoursed at length of poison, being especially learned on the subject. Rubbing his hands together respectfully, while his eyes, shrewd and wholly dissociated from the gesture, gazed sharply at them, he talked of Crateuas, who had been attached to the court of Mithridates Eupator of Pontus, and of the treatise on poisonous plants which Crateuas had written for the King. The doctor's eyes gleamed with enthusiasm now. Mithridates had favoured poison in assisting his enemies from this life; he had ransacked the world for poisons, for antidotes as well. The doctor mentioned hemlock and belladonna. Then aconitum.

For Lucius, there had been no struggle at the end. He had lain as if asleep, his face at peace, as beautiful in death as in life. But . . . he had died. The only poison which would produce peaceful death was aconite. They were familiar with it? Aconite acted on the heart, producing a gradual slowing down and asphyxia. The plant grew in Crete and Zakynthos, but the best specimens were to be found at Heraklea in Pontus. The poison came from the root of the plant and uncommon skill and knowledge were needed to extract it and to regulate the dose. If drunk mixed in wine or a honey posset it could not be tasted. It could be so compounded as to prove fatal at a given moment—the longer the elapsed time, the more painful the death. If it acted at once, death would be quite painless. No antidote had ever been discovered. The dose administered to Lucius, then, had been just the correct amount to produce death within only a few hours.

All this could only make them more anxious. *Venenum!* Magic spell or poison—one and the same thing, as everyone knew. The same word embraced both. She who used magic spells would—it went without saying—also use poison, a poison such as this versatile and rare exotic, favoured by the connoisseur.

Something niggled at the back of Fufidius' mind after they saw the doctor. Aconite . . . from Heraklea Pontica. At home again, he went to his library and pulled out one roll after another. He found what he wanted. Then he stayed motionless for a long time, reading the contents of the roll.

This was a poem addressed to King Mithridates which had been written by Cinna during his service in Bithynia with the forces of Pompeius Magnus. Precious, intricate and brilliant, it pondered—in elegant choliambics—Mithridates' defeat and the end fit for so cultured and so cruel a potentate, himself an expert poisoner. Death by poison it would be, of course, for such a sophisticate, but death painless as well, swift and sure for this man who had fallen between two worlds, east and west, and who had loved Greek culture. There was a flower—a beautiful flower, blue-helmeted, which grew luxuriant and wild in Pontic Heraklea, the root of which was like in shape and colour to a prawn and which, if compounded with sufficient artistry, would render death painless. The poison was aconite. . . .

Fufidius saw, by the design on a corner of the scroll, that the poem had lately been copied by a scribe of Eucharis. In order to write that poem, Cinna had certainly learned about aconite. Might he even have brought back a quantity of the precious substance from Bithynia? He had ruthlessly ridiculed Lucius in public. Could he have dealt him the death blow at the banquet? Wasn't poison, refined and sure, administered during the reading of a poem about a girl's betrayal by a man—what Cinna obviously feared for Fufidia? Wasn't such a poison just what a Cinna would choose to procure an artistic death?

But then, if it had been Cinna, would he let his sister stand trial? It was not impossible, if he and Helvia had acted together, because of her admiration for her brother and his career. Helvia could not be moved, once she had her mind made up.

Why had Cinna been so concerned for Fufidia? Had he . . . but Fufidius' mind boggled at incest. This was . . . incredible. Affection between brother and sister there had always been. An unnatural relationship? He could not believe it. This was not, in any case, a time for such questions. It was a time for family solidarity. And to this course, grimly, Fufidius was committing himself.

They were the worst days Helvia had ever known: interminable days, even while the date of the trial marched inexorably towards her. Mostly she stayed indoors. It was the time of the Parentalia, when Romans honoured their dead. But Helvia was far from her family's tomb. She stayed at home while the others went in a body to make their offerings at the tomb of that Fufidius who had been Propraetor of Hispania Ulterior. There also were the remains of Fufidius' father. Besides, it was not prudent for an accused woman to be seen in public.

Fufidius was busy nowadays calling in loans and amassing cash in order to have ample money for bribes and for financing Helvia's flight if she were found guilty. But none of them could think of this possibility. Outlawed and "cut off from the fire and water of her tribe," where would she go as an exile? Who would take her in and how would she survive, banished from all her dear ones? It was unthinkable.

This afternoon Helvia—supposedly—was resting after a session with Cicero. He had been sympathetic and she had found it a relief to talk. He had made her go over all the events leading up to the banquet and every detail of it. She had even remembered to bring with her Lucius' jewelled dice-box which he had left behind in the dining room after the banquet. Family details were given in full. Cicero was painstaking in this preparation, though he would give no hint of the defence he would present. Helvia felt that he thought her guilty.

Although Cicero had put new heart in them all, today this painstaking recall of the past was having the paradoxical effect of making Helvia far less confident of the outcome of the trial. She had resorted to magic for the sake of her daughter. Should she be found guilty of murder, her exile—if it were permitted— although heavy to bear, would still be much less of a burden to her than the nightmarish knowledge of the shame she had brought on her family. Not even Cinna, Tribune though he was, would escape ignominy. Fufidia could not possibly make a good marriage. The career prospects of young Quintus would be blighted. Her husband would suffer. All but a fraction of Helvia's estate would be forfeited for the benefit of the accursed Scauri.

The case which Marcus Scaurus would present was so plausible. Helvia was reasoning now, in a clear, matter-of-fact way. Any outsider would accept without question that Lucius Scaurus had been poisoned at her banquet. And she, the hostess and the organiser, was the one who had had the greatest, almost the only chance of administering the poison. Everyone knew she opposed the marriage. She had made little effort, beyond what formality itself required, to hide her feelings. Even worse, her dabbling in magic was known and would be brought against her, thanks to her husband's shouting and stamping after he found evidence of it in the garden. All the slaves must know. It was easy to see how this information had leaked to the Scauri. Consorting with a witch was a crime almost as serious as murder itself. At least the witch had not been seen by the slaves. As for the charge of incest, she did not know how it could be substantiated. Surely Scaurus was going too far here? It could rebound on him.

Longing for Cinna flooded through her. Not only his public duties but prudence also kept him away these days. The thought of him prompted Helvia to do something which she had not done for many years. She sought out a carefully wrapped and sealed dozen or so pages of manuscript which she always kept locked away with her family jewels, secret even from her husband and children. These were love poems written to her by her brother in those years just before and after her marriage to Fufidius, a marriage forced on her by her family. Her memory sped back to her early teens and the wild exuberant passion of brother and sister which had crowned their childhood attachment, which had the dangerous lure of the illicit.

She crouched trembling on her bed for a long time. Then she shook herself and sprang up, snatching a polished bronze mirror to inspect her reflection. She scowled at what she saw. Her hair added to her misery nowadays. It had always been thick and luxuriant. And so it still looked, but only Helvia knew how carefully it had to be brushed forward on her brow. A high forehead was all very well, but her hair was receding in alarming fashion.

To comfort herself, she unwrapped the small packet which she had taken out of the locked chest and unrolled the manuscripts. They were in chronological order. She had always been orderly. She set herself to forget her worries just for a little and began to read the poems through, slowly and appreciatively. They came from the greatest living Roman poet and once more she savoured the fire and delicacy of that bond between them. Her eyes grew dreamy as she remembered the last of the private poems Cinna had dedicated to her before she had insisted on his writing for public readings. . . .

Helvia started violently. Feverishly she checked through each of the manuscripts. That last and very sexually explicit poem was missing! Panic took hold of her, clutching her throat and breast, darkening her vision.

Later, she realised that she must have fainted for the first time in her life. When she recovered, she knew that her mind was made up. That poem, which could only have been taken by someone who wished her ill, would now certainly be made available to Marcus Scaurus. For a good price, of course. This was too much. Faced with this evidence of her behaviour, no jury would believe her anything but infamous—a woman capable of any crime. Add this to all the other evidence and how damning the cumulative effect would be! She *must* be found guilty! Her property would be confiscated and her burial forbidden. All things pointed to the logical, inexorable conclusion. There must not be a trial!

For a long time Helvia sat there, and then she set about her preparations composedly and efficiently. That night she insisted that her son and daughter should go to bed early. She checked that Gratidia was already asleep. It was a relief to put thought aside. Strength she had now and energy that came from a resolution based on reason. She kissed both her children tenderly, and steeling herself to appear normal, briskly sent them off. Fufidius was not at home. Probably he was with Eucharis. Helvia took a wax tablet and wrote him a note.

"It is better for our family that I take this course. I leave them in your capable hands. This way, my testament will be respected."

Finally, she wrote to Cinna.

"My dearest brother, you will understand and forgive the weakness of a woman who loves but cannot face shame."

Then Helvia burnt the remaining poems.

The slaves filled her bath with hot and aromatic water, and she dismissed them, saying she wanted to be alone and would put herself to bed. She lay down, slashed her wrists, and watching the blood stain the water, felt herself sinking into unconsciousness.

She did not see the hesitant head of her favourite maid, urged on by Cinna, peer round a softly opened door. Nor hear the scream of the woman and the voice of her brother, swift and incisive, using the rudimentary medical knowledge of all educated Romans and applying makeshift tourniquets to her arms.

A doctor was hastily called. He was bribed to secrecy. He bound her arms and pronounced her safe. She would be weak for several days, but that was all. Fufidia and Quintus were still asleep. Cinna settled down to watch over his sister as she slowly recovered consciousness.

Only when he was sure that Helvia fully understood him, did Cinna tell her that evidence had come to light of a visit made by Lucius Scaurus on his way to the banquet. During this visit he had drunk wine. There had been every opportunity for Lucius to be poisoned in the course of this visit. Cicero, he added, was very satisfied with this new evidence.

XXI

It was on them at last, the 25th of February—the day fixed for the trial. It was to begin at a cruelly early hour. Helvia had spent the night wide-eyed, staring into the darkness, falling into a half sleep in the hour before dawn, to be jerked from her uneasy dreams by an anxious-eyed Fufidius. So long had she waited for the shish-shish of the door, the whispered warning to wake and be ready, that now in her exhaustion the flickering lamps in the dark, the grey shapes of her serving women as they dressed her seemed to belong to some other time than the present.

By first light they were jolting over the paving stones in a closed carriage, Helvia crammed in with her husband and son and daughter, their nerves tingling with apprehension for what was to come that day, working through that dazed feeling that had been upon them ever since the first summons. The dawn wind had died and the sun came up, sending waves of misty light over the already bustling city. They had to descend from the carriage in the Forum and walk the last part along the Via Sacra to the Basilica Aemilia where the trial was to be held. Veiled to the eyes, with Fufidius keeping a tight hold of her on one side, Quintus on the other, Helvia felt her shoulders and spine taut as she trod the stones under the curious eyes of the Roman mob—businessmen and clerks and officials, unkept workers, idlers and shopkeepers. She saw no hint of compassion in their staring faces, so many of them vitiated and deprived, stupid or cynical or hopeless—but all of them curious.

"If only my darling child could have stayed at home," moaned Helvia. For Fufidia had had to come. The presence of the whole family in court was important. She followed now with Gratidia and a small nucleus of trusted servants.

They passed under the colonnades of the Basilica, the great Corinthian columns of black, red and white African marble tow-

ering above them. The *iudex quaestionis* or president of the court
had had his tribunal set up in a far corner. Fufidius' party took
their places on the benches set for them before the tribunal.
Opposite, the prosecution lawyers were already conferring, and
before long the large body of judges settled in their seats on the
tribunal. Someone blew a blast on a trumpet and the presiding
judge entered, an imposing figure, to seat himself on his ivory
chair of curule office.

Hundreds of spectators noisily thronged the sides of the court,
drawn by rumours of scandal in high society and curious to observe the unusual spectacle of a wealthy woman arraigned for
murder. But the fifty-strong body of judges could expect only a
long day of concentration on sophisticated argument. Those few
judges who had taken bribes from both the Aemilii Scauri and
the Fufidii hoped for the appearance of an even balance in the
presentations. Fufidius, drawing freely on wealth, had not stinted
the sum thus invested. Roughly half the jury were of equestrian
rank like Fufidius, half of senatorial rank like Scaurus.

The bereaved clan of the Scauri were clad in the deepest
mourning and the men had let their hair grow. A grim-faced
Marcus Scaurus was seen often to clench his hands and members
of the family wept from time to time, in quiet and restrained
fashion. Helvia also wore a mourning garment, though she
scorned to weep. Her family, ranged on either side of her, followed the conventions of the day in their dishevelled appearance, little Fufidia especially drawing sympathetic murmurs, her
fair beauty only enhanced by the black of her stole, her gorgeous
blond hair tumbling over her shoulders.

The judges were sworn in, and the Aemilii Scauri were called
on to begin their case. The hubbub quickly died as the audience
waited to see how the charge of murder would be introduced.

Marcus Scaurus, himself once an advocate of talent, spoke
first. He had a good strong voice and commanding presence. He
was dignified and vivid. He raised sympathy in all who heard
him. His listeners tasted his agony as a father at the death of his
younger son. Lucius, descendant of that noble house, grandson
of the famous consul, had been a young officer of promise who
would shortly have left for duty in the coming war against the
Parthians.

Many in the audience remembered the splendour of Marcus Scaurus' shows, the theatre he had built, his munificence to the people of Rome as aedile fourteen years before. They heard him attentively as he spoke now of his family's frenzied, sick questionings after Lucius' death. Who could have been responsible? No man alive was without enemies. The court was familiar with Scaurus' own career. Inevitable that he had made a few enemies. But none had been at the banquet after which his son had died.

It had become, outside, a day of warm promise, with a tremulous breath of spring in the air, and a tender blue sky that seemed ready to burst into tears. Whiffs of perfume from sweet plants drifted in to play on the senses. Waves of anger and sorrow came easily to the crowd that morning. Marcus Scaurus' grief became their own.

"The young can be high-spirited, sometimes over-hasty in words, Lucius no less than others. But who would have wished him dead?" Marcus Scaurus asked. Accidental poisoning was out of the question. No other guest had been affected. The Scauri had been driven, against their will, to consider members of Fufidius' family. Quintus Fufidius had made the marriage agreement with enthusiasm, with delight. *His* hand in Lucius' death was not to be thought of. But his wife—ah, Helvia. As the following speaker for the prosecution would confirm, Helvia had gradually been revealed as the logical, indeed the only one, who could have committed the dreadful crime. As he stood down, Marcus Scaurus gave way to bitter grief. Angry rumblings came from the crowd and were not easily silenced.

Judge and audience had ample time to savour the anguish of the father. After a well-timed wait Decimus Scaurus, second speaker for the prosecution, rose. He might come from a minor branch of the family, but the name and the implied connections were of help. He dealt at length with the facts of the crime, described the banquet, the guests, the entertainment. Lucius had spent the day at home; he had gone to a banquet where only intimates and relatives were present. Who could have poisoned him if not one of the Fufidii, some of whom, indeed, were hostile to Lucius, one of whom—on the reasonable evidence of their own eyes and ears—had hated him. At such a banquet, who would find it easier than the hostess to drop poison into a cup, under cover of the rapt attention given by all to the jugglers, or to the lengthy poetry-play which was then enacted?

Indeed, he could tell them that Helvia was away from the banquet for a good half hour, undoubtedly the time when she brought the carefully prepared poison. Her absence was commented on by Marcus Scaurus, who had dined next to her; he had even been affronted at her lack of courtesy. It was not the first time he had had to bear with such behaviour from her. From the time of his first meeting with her, he had noticed a coldness of manner, a disinclination to talk, a reluctance to respond to any attempt of his son Lucius to please her. He had thought that on such an occasion as this she might have managed to hide her feelings.

Now, it was after Helvia's return to the dining room that Lucius' pallor had first been noticed by several people. The poison, as they would later hear from the family doctor of the Scauri, was very probably aconite, a poison which needed no little expertise to compound, but which if administered by some knowledgeable person, could be made to act at a given moment.

That there was every reason for Helvia—this model of rectitude—to have such knowledge, would be shown later. For she, of seemingly impeccable character, wife of this worthy townsman of Arpinum, was not what she seemed. He would leave it to the final speaker for the prosecution to tell the court just what manner of woman the accused was. . . .

Decimus Scaurus had effectively prepared the ground for revelations to come. Amid eager expectations, Marcus Valerius Messalla, noble, talented, distinguished, rose to make the main speech for the prosecution. The young man was considered to be an orator of the first order. Cicero knew him for a worthy opponent.

"It is with sadness, gentlemen, that I charge Helvia with the murder of Lucius Scaurus. Her family, although not illustrious, is worthy and its men have given good service to the state. And it is a grievous matter to have to charge a wife and mother with such a bestial act as murder. But on this occasion the case is clearcut. Motive, opportunity and character—all point inescapably to Helvia.

"Let me begin with motive. This was hostility to the young

noble whom Helvia's husband had been so delighted to wel-
come as son-in-law. And who was welcomed with delight, I
should tell you, by the girl herself. The fact of Helvia's hostility
is no secret. All her friends and family knew of it; it had so taken
over her mind that this willful and headstrong woman did not
conceal it from the family of the Scauri, even when formal courtesy demanded it. She loved as strongly as she hated, and her
devotion to her daughter was widely remarked upon. Further-
more, she made no secret of her anger at the action of her good
husband, Quintus Fufidius, in making this contract without consulting her, despite the fact that it was a far better marriage than
she could herself have arranged. Day after day she harangued
and pleaded with him to repudiate the marriage contract. It is
said that at the same time she and another member of her family
—I shall have more to tell you on this later—were making enquiries elsewhere for a husband for her daughter. In brief, judges,
this woman frantically sought to prevent the marriage of her
daughter with the young noble Lucius Scaurus.

"And now . . ." He paused and the crowd swelled, scenting
lurid disclosures. "And now I can tell you of the intensity of her
obsession—yes, obsession is not too strong a word—when she
realised that only the removal of the young man would stop the
marriage taking place." His voice rang out on a note of horror.
"Gentlemen, this woman resorted to spells. Criminal act though
it is for magic to be invoked, for this deeply offends our gods,
Helvia's obsession pushed her to that extreme. How do we
know of this? I will tell you. Quite by chance, it seems, her
husband discovered one day the disgusting evidence of a magic
spell, the gutted body of a small dead creature, hanging from a
tree at the east end of their garden. A typical magic spell for
death. The honest Fufidius was enraged to find that such evil had
been done in his own garden, and that it could only have been
done by his wife. Nobody else would have dared. His shouted
remonstrances, his legitimate anger, were heard by the whole
household.

"It is not difficult, gentlemen, to deduce the target of this
spell. Lucius Scaurus, of course! And were I to ask Fufidius to
confirm this, he—honourable man as he is—would undoubtedly
tell you so. But I would not wish to place him in the invidious

position of giving testimony which could only publicly confirm the wickedness of his wife. Nor, under our system of law, could he be forced to do so.

"Motive for the crime there certainly was, then. And also opportunity, as my colleague Decimus Scaurus has pointed out. The young man was poisoned at the banquet of the Fufidii. He was at home all that day and indeed not even the most reckless advocate for the defence would suggest that he ingested poison in his own family home. He was well when he went to the reception; he was dead soon after. We can conclude only that he was given poison during the course of the evening. Who but Helvia made arrangements for the food and drink? Consider the opportunities, when passing Lucius Scaurus, to slip poison in his cup while his attention was distracted by the entertainment. Ah, the entertainment! Arranged specially for this purpose, I will assert to you. At what a point in the proceedings did the young man begin to feel unwell! How carefully had Helvia chosen the setting: first the troupe of jugglers, forcing, with their skill and action, the concentration of the guests; then the poetry-play, so colourfully performed by M. Ofilius Hilarus' company of actors —that poetry-play-within-a-play, giving the story of Theseus and Ariadne. Lucius Scaurus swallowed that poison which did him brutally to death just when the chorus bemoaned the desertion of Ariadne by Theseus. Oh, evil artistry! Is it not clear that Helvia expected Lucius to betray her daughter—"

"Not before he got through the dowry though!" yelled a spectator, and there was a titter of laughter from those near.

"It is not clear that she expected this, though there was no reason for her to think so from his previous behaviour? . . ."

A restless muttering came from the ring of listeners. Knowing the struggle was between rival ingenuities, they were still waiting to separate the true from the untrue. Sternly, the *iudex* called for order.

"It was her diseased imagination which prompted her to poison Lucius Scaurus," declared Messalla. "Can you not *see* her quick, pleased look the instant after the wine is drunk, when the die is irrevocably cast, the opportunity taken?

"And finally, character. Judges, only a woman of black depravity could poison a young noble deeply in love with her beautiful daughter and equally loved in return."

Messalla paused again. This time the audience, sensing a climax to his address, fell utterly silent. Even the chatter of attendants gaming in the portico seemed to hush. Helvia, white-faced but impassive, longed for Cinna, who had been requested by Cicero not to attend. Fufidius' hand was over hers, but she felt no current of rapport with him.

"Oh, judges, I tell you that this woman—intelligent, willful and passionate—is far from being the conventional and trustworthy Roman matron she appears to the world. I have already underlined her implacable opposition to her husband's wishes. Not for her to conform, oh no. Nor in other ways does she conform. Not for Helvia the devotion to her household gods, not for her the religious observance that is the duty of women and the strength of our society. I regret to tell you, gentlemen, that Helvia is a devotee of that Egyptian goddess, that Isis, whose worship has so many times been banned from our city— was forbidden, indeed, as recently as four years ago."

The advocate paused, glancing at the judges, singling out L. Aemilius Paullus in particular.

"You will remember how one of your number, when Consul, once tore off his toga and drove an axe through the temple doors to set an example to the workmen who had been told to demolish the Iseum. Anyone will applaud such an example who is a true Roman and faithful to the gods who protect our state."

The speaker could ignore the waves of muted protest rising from angry spectators now, so many of whom were humble folk. None of the judges, all coming from that comfortably enshrined noble or knightly class, upheld such worship. All the same, he was on delicate ground. Caesar was in power and Caesar had reinstated Isis.

"Imported worship which deals not in solemn rites owed to traditional gods, but in mysteries and frenzies and incited enthusiasms," rumbled the advocate ominously. "Why would a lady of Helvia's class and background have recourse to such practices?

"I do not ask you what can happen in the temple of linen-clad Isis, gentlemen," he went on ironically. "I do not care to ask you —nor, judges, would you particularly wish to know. But we do

know that in other towns the shrines of that goddess are gener-
ally not too far from the brothels, and we are content to remain
in ignorance of those who give their devotion to bulls and monkeys and reptiles and birds of all sorts and," Messalla paused
delicately, his face a nice study in lofty distaste, "those who are
said to indulge in practices erotic or magical . . .

"Helvia's resort to Isis worship, to magic, is alien to women of
her status. Who can trust a woman who covertly enlists the
forces of darkness and evil? She who does so is clearly capable of
any deed. But this is not all . . ."

Messalla paused again.

"As we all know, the great bulwark of our community, its
whole strength, is the family, by reason of its natural and human
ties. As we all know, the greatest merit of all from the family is
this union of man and woman for the procreation of children.

"I do not argue that Helvia was not a devoted mother." Another pause. Messalla looked around for absolute quiet now and
waited till he got it. "I do not argue that, *iudices*. I argue only
that Helvia was, as well, too devoted a sister. This woman, married to the honest Fufidius for almost twenty years now, since she
was fifteen years old, has for long had a most delightful relationship with her brother. With her brother Cinna, the poet, who is
now also Tribune. I regret, however, that it is a most unnatural
relationship as well. I speak, gentlemen, of an incestuous relationship."

A long collective sigh rose from the audience. This was better
than any theatre. Helvia sat as if turned to stone, her mature
beauty etched in the band of light that fell on the bench. Aghast,
Fufidius half rose to his feet, but was motioned down by Cicero.

"This relationship may have been suspected by a few, but it
was well hidden by the incestuous pair. As you know, slaves
cannot testify against their masters except in one instance—in a
case of incest. Permission was requested in this case. Helvia's
husband refused to have his slaves questioned. We had, necessarily, to accept this refusal."

Messalla was all elegance. If he lacked real fire, the very matter of his scandalous disclosures more than made up for it.

"And from the coupling of brother and sister," the barrister let drop the remark casually, "was born Helvia's daughter Fufidia, fair as her mother is fair."

An angry and thunderous protest burst from the audience as they heard of this crime against the gods. When the noise finally died away, the advocate continued.

"If anyone should doubt this, *iudices,* I have proof. I have proof because a poet is always a poet." He waved a manuscript. "This is a poem entitled *Ad Helviam.* I need read you only the first lines . . ." And he read:

> "Ad Helviam
> Sister wife, my love's delight
> Fruitful womb, our pledge this night . . ."

"These lines are, you will agree, sufficiently conclusive when addressed to a woman with one brother, a poet. The remaining lines are a scandalous exaltation of their passion. Ah, judges, is it not all clear? This woman, whose conduct is far beyond all limits of even the most depraved society, is desperate to keep under her direction the daughter born of her incestuous relationship. The plans which she and her brother had for their daughter's marriage, the continued possessiveness they no doubt imply, are not to be upset. There is no boundary to what such a woman will try. She has years of lying and deceit behind her. A readiness to employ the proscribed art of magic does not bring results. So direct action must be taken. The end is death. Gentlemen! Conviction and punishment must follow!"

Messalla sat down to a tumult of shouts and applause.

XXII

There was a brief interchange between members of the defending counsel after Messalla sat down. Cicero's head stayed close to that of young Quintus Fufidius during the speech of Q. Arrius, who opened the case for the defence. Arrius, an experienced young advocate from Minturnae, son of a neighbour of Cicero's at his Formiae villa, began in a conversational tone which quietly lessened the sense of drama introduced by Messalla.

"Your ears must still be tingling—and in unpleasant fashion—at the appalling charges levelled at my client, *iudices.* I doubt very much—indeed I am sure—that no one person, certainly no woman, has ever appeared in this court and listened to such a savage and relentless blackening of her character and reputation as has my client. So utter a monster has the prosecution painted Helvia, so fiendish a schemer, so vindictive, so wanton in her behaviour, that even the most gullible listeners of the tirade can scarcely believe in it all!"

Arrius, who looked completely relaxed, almost laughed at this point, in ironical fashion. He was a big man with a big voice, and always commanded attention.

"And if any one of these charges be false," he demanded, "is there a reason why the others cannot also be false? Let me confine myself then to a single charge. Helvia is said to be a worshipper of Isis. We were given no proof whatsoever of this, but even if she were, would such a thing prove Helvia's lack of morals? Our empire, gentlemen, has come into being partly because of our success in assimilating other races in a wise fashion. We have rarely enforced more than a nominal submission from those we have conquered, but have allowed them to continue to worship as they please and to retain their own local institutions. It is a source of our power. So it is with our treatment of foreigners who have crossed to our city. It is the reason for foreign cults being allowed. Only when there was risk of political manipulation of the worshippers have the shrines of any outside deity been forbidden. It has been our custom to allow them to take their place alongside the traditional gods of the Roman people. Thus our objection has not been to the worship of Isis as such, but to the dangers of her gatherings being infiltrated by subversive elements.

"Even now, you must all be aware that the temple of Isis has again been reopened and the worship that was a few years ago driven into private houses has again come out into the open.

"So even if Helvia were proved to be a worshipper, she would be doing no wrong. But in fact the allegation is simply untrue. It rests on evidence so slight as to be no evidence at all! Let me tell you of the acquaintance of Helvia with Isis. It consists of a visit to the temple of Isis while Helvia was in Pompeii some months ago, when she spent several weeks in the company—indeed, in the house—of a very dear relative of hers, a lady whose husband is a retired magistrate and member of the equestrian order, a man who has taken up his residence in Pompeii, who is the owner of a well-appointed, even luxurious villa, and who is enjoying the last years of his life in that pleasant and cultivated town. In the course of this visit Helvia was conducted around the main sights of the town, and she brought back many little mementos of her stay. A little oil lamp with an effigy of the goddess was one of her purchases. This kind of thing is turned out by an army of artisans for the visitor or passing sightseer; outside temples, votive offerings are sold, outside great buildings, you will find copies of works of art. We have all seen tourist stalls, judges. It is to be hoped that the next time you or I purchase some pretty object for our wife—a piece of purple cloth, an anklet—she will not be branded a prostitute for the possession of it!"

Quintus Arrius talked on easily and entertainingly for some time until a little nod from Cicero caused him to end his speech gracefully. He had done good service to the defence in giving the *patronus* the chance to work over the unexpected evidence of Cinna's poem that had been hurled at them. But everyone knew that the whole defence case was in the balance.

Helvia stared fascinated at her son Quintus conferring with

Cicero. Ever since the poem had been read out, the proceedings of the trial had blurred into a nightmare. She could no longer think clearly. She was hardly conscious of little Fufidia clutching her hand consolingly.

Quintus Fufidius rose to speak, young, handsome, passionately convinced of what he had to say. He stood before the judges squarely on his two feet, his head thrown back, his hands at his sides. He was to use them rarely. His case was too serious, his emotion too genuine, for oratorical tricks.

He was highly nervous at his first speech in court, but he began bravely, testing his voice against the vastness of the hall, his training standing firm behind him now, as he used all his taught artistry in reaching every one of the spectators grouped in a ring about the tribunal. He felt the curious eyes of each one of the large body of judges boring into him from the platform. Seldom, if ever, had they seen a son as counsel for the defence of his mother.

"As you know, *iudices,* the defendant is my mother. I have listened, my family has listened, while the prosecution have painted a foul picture of her. We have heard that she murdered by poison the fiancé of her beloved daughter at a banquet—she, who has watched so carefully over the slaves who prepared food and drink of our family for the entire course of our lives.

"She is immoral, I am told, she who all through my life has continuously been the mainstay of our home, who taught her children the value of right living in all its aspects. She is immoral, so they say, she who from our earliest years has been a shining example of all a good mother should be!"

The hall quietened and Quintus, almost forgetting his audience, gave himself to impassioned persuasion, the sonorous Latin periods falling from his lips with weight and point.

"Looking back to my childhood in Arpinum, I have the happiest memories. We had a large family of farm workers and house servants, and you will learn that not one can be found who would not vouch for the kindness of my mother in every respect. In the case of illness or injury she was always at hand, and many a woman suffering the pangs of childbirth, many a woman who fell sick, was glad of the personal attention which my mother, who ministered so gently to them, could offer. My father is beloved for the services he rendered to the townspeople, for the entertainments he offered. My mother is loved and respected not only as his wife but in her own right.

"My mother was not born in Arpinum. She comes from the north. She comes from Brixia, where she and her brother, the tribune Cinna, grew up on the estate of my grandfather in a community both hardworking and thrifty, where honest dealing and traditional morality are held dear. These characteristics my mother brought to her marriage with my father. My sister and I, gentlemen, had a mother who knew and valued all that is best in municipal life. It is this beloved mother whom I now see accused of these *ludicrous* crimes. I think you can imagine, gentlemen, the feelings of my little sister and myself, our sickness and shock that our mother should be said to have indulged herself in vile and unnatural fashion with our dear uncle, of whom she is fond indeed, but fond in the most innocent of ways."

The audience followed Quintus' gaze. Sympathetic murmurs rose as they too looked at the piteous, beautiful young girl seated beside her mother. All felt the most righteous of anger on her behalf.

"I could tell you so much more, gentlemen. I could talk indefinitely and still not do justice to Helvia's sweetness and virtue. I could read you her letters to me when I studied in Athens— letters so charming, so wise, so full of loving advice that I will always treasure them . . . But now I must read you certain testimonials from other persons . . ."

Quintus, one eye on Cicero, read from a sheaf of papers. All the testimonials came from prominent Arpinates, from friends and colleagues and employees. Quintus began to read slowly, speeding up when Cicero gave the signal that he was ready to begin his own discourse. The young man finished on an urgent note. The accusers were wildly wrong and all these good people could not be mistaken. The judges must see by now that the charges were utterly misplaced. . . .

XXIII

Slowly, Cicero rose to speak.

"I have not practised in the courts for some time," he began in a calm, ordered manner which was itself an appeal to reason. "But several considerations impelled me to defend Helvia. I have known the family of the Fufidii for many years. Helvia's husband, Quintus Fufidius, was my valued military tribune in Cilicia, ánd thus closely associated with me. I had every opportunity to observe in him that high degree of efficiency, honesty and concern for the problems he faced there which I had expected of him. He is a good man, strong in his religious observance, in his love for his family and care for his children. Qualities, indeed, present in the whole family. Helvia is an exemplary wife and the mother of two lovely children. The son is serious and scholarly, as you will have gathered by his speech, so much so in fact that I myself have taken him as a pupil. The daughter is beautiful and obedient to her mother as she prepares for womanhood."

Cicero paused, his words echoing sonorously in a hall now almost completely quiet.

"And this wife, this mother, is the selfsame lady arraigned before you on a charge which, as I shall easily show you, is as shameful as it is baseless.

"And I am defending Helvia not only because she is completely innocent, but also in memory of my own dear daughter. It is through her that I have been made keenly aware of the difficulties which a woman faces when we men decide to act without due thought, when we are mistaken and strike at the weaker rather than the stronger. This is the trap into which the Aemilii Scauri have fallen, gentlemen. Theirs is a family once greatly renowned, which produced that Scaurus who was chief of the Senate and political oracle of his order, immortalized as well as the originator of some of our principal public buildings and works. Their name will live forever in one of our great consular roads. But all families can be misled into believing the unbelievable, into seeking a wrongful vengeance based on superficial plausibility."

Cicero judged that he had by now changed the atmosphere in which the trial was being held into a lower key. People would less easily accept now that a woman of Helvia's background should suddenly have acted so fiendishly out of character. He wanted also to prepare for a later contrast in tone.

"The prosecution has made much of Helvia's possessiveness towards her daughter, of her wish to have a hand in the choice of a husband. I am sure this is true—and is it not equally true of your wives, gentlemen? Show me a mother not concerned with her daughter's welfare and with the man she marries, and you will show me an unnatural—not a perfectly normal—mother like Helvia. We can scarcely claim it as a motive for murder.

"And then there was supposed to be some mumbo-jumbo of magic and a husband shouting at his wife. We were never shown the mumbo-jumbo. Are we to believe, gentlemen, that a woman of refinement, of education, sister of an honoured poet, would have descended to making spells! To dealing in dead animals! Not a shred of proof backs up this assertion. And again, gentlemen," and Cicero laughed with gentle deprecation, "who amongst us has not shouted at his wife? Is a wife who provokes a husband to shout at her thereby proved to have murderous intentions? No, the usual disagreements between husband and wife cannot be blown up into an indication of her moral delinquency. To suggest it is enough to see the absurdity.

"Gentlemen, have you ever seen pictured in a still pool of water the definite formation of the hills and the sky surrounding it? How permanent such a picture looks. Yet interrupt the pool only slightly, question the durability of the picture with a tossed pebble and the whole picture breaks up and disappears. In the same way, my few gentle questions, tossed at the prosecution's picture of motives bring the same result—the picture disappears."

Murmurs of appreciation of this verbal deftness could be heard from the audience, which by now had so increased that people were standing far down the nave. Fortunately, no other trials were being held in the Basilica at that time, so the speaker was clearly audible.

"And now opportunity," Cicero continued in the same conversational tone. "Yes, it does seem that Helvia had opportunity. As the prosecution rightly observed, she as hostess was continually moving amongst her guests and she must have been within reach of Lucius Scaurus a number of times. So, I suppose, must a number of the guests also. Impossible, of course, that one of these could have harboured a grudge against the unfortunate young man! Or that one of the slaves could have been bribed by someone not even present to slip poison into his wine?" Cicero's voice hardened. "I have heard that the young man made enemies as enthusiastically as he made love. So you must concede that the hostess of a banquet after which a guest dies must not necessarily be held responsible."

Young Quintus Fufidius and Arrius, alone of all the multitude present, knew what was happening. Cicero, outwardly so confident and masterly, if restrained, played for time while he planned what response he would make to the damning poem which the prosecution had sprung on them.

"Of course, had Lucius gone out of his home," Cicero was gathering himself for an assault now, "had Lucius gone out before leaving for the banquet, there would be greater doubt still. There would have been opportunity for a person as yet unknown to have administered poison which took effect only later. Such delayed impacts are well known. If I could show that Lucius Scaurus did in fact have such an encounter with others, opportunity could no longer be pointed as a spear at the breast of my client. But you heard my learned colleague for the prosecution, Marcus Valerius Messalla, say that Lucius Scaurus was in the family home all day prior to leaving for the Fufidii banquet."

With great deliberation Cicero continued, after a pause in which tension mounted perceptibly.

"He was wrong. Wrong in this statement as he was in his distorted representation of motive. I have incontrovertible proof that this is so. What proof, you ask? I shall tell you."

Cicero went on to tell an attentive court that he had been visited only the day before by Marcus Furius Bibaculus, who had been unexpectedly recalled to Rome after setting out for Africa recently on the staff of the newly appointed Governor of Africa, Vetus. While Bibaculus was in Rome, he was a regular attender at the poetry gatherings which took place at the house of a certain woman Eucharis, who had attained some notoriety as the supervisor of a small publishing business. The afternoon before Bibaculus left, he went to her house to leave there two poems which he could not read himself at the next gathering because of his forthcoming absence from Rome.

"You will hear his evidence later on—trustworthy evidence from a man who combines literary and military prowess in a special way. You may know that an epic poem was recently written by the same Bibaculus on the Gallic campaign of Julius Caesar. I believe that one of the poems which he left for copying was this very one. Fortunate we are that great deeds of mighty commanders and their armies may be properly recorded and celebrated for history."

The president of the court smiled to himself at the neat insertion of public praise for Caesar.

"And, gentlemen, while Furius Bibaculus was in the house of this Eucharis on the afternoon of the very day of the Fufidii banquet, who should arrive? Yes, you anticipate me. It was none other than Lucius Scaurus, the same young man who—we have been told—was at home all day. Let us look further at this visit, which apparently was not known to the prosecution. Of course, as I said, it destroys their account of opportunity. Now why did Scaurus visit Eucharis that day? True, he knew her and I understand had even read a very vivid poem at one of the gatherings, though it was written by another."

There were only half-concealed grins from several of the men on the jury, who appreciatively recalled the spectacle of a Scaurus induced to ridicule himself publicly.

"We might say it was a social visit. Perhaps the young man wished to contrast Greek beauty with the Roman beauty of his future wife, whom he would shortly be seeing. We cannot know for sure. The dead take their secrets—guilty as well as innocent —to the grave. But we do have two witnesses—Marcus Furius Bibaculus and the woman Eucharis. The young soldier-poet tells me he was puzzled by the talk, at one point, between Lucius Scaurus and Eucharis. He realised that they knew each other well, although they did not seem intimate. Lucius Scaurus kept referring to an interest that the two of them had in common, without actually putting into words what it was. It also seemed to be linked to a beautiful jewelled dice-box which Scaurus picked up in the salon. The young man idly diced as the three of them talked. That—"Cicero's voice rose in emphasis, "that was the dice-box found in the house of the Fufidii after the banquet— under the couch on which Lucius Scaurus had reclined." With a flourish, Cicero held up the rich little object.

"My witness confirms that he and Lucius were, of course, offered wine. But he tells me that the wine given Lucius Scaurus came from a different bowl, and when he asked Eucharis if he might try it, she avoided offering it to him.

"Gentlemen, now we have not only an undisclosed visit by Lucius Scaurus just prior to his attendance at the banquet, but also the fact, witnessed and testified, that the other guest of Eucharis was not permitted to drink the wine taken by Lucius Scaurus. And finally, the puzzling episode of a valuable jewelled dice-box which Scaurus obviously took with him from Eucharis' place. What explanation can there by for this apparent transfer of a valuable object from a young Greek woman to Scaurus? To my mind there is only one explanation. Judges—with your permission and that of the prosecutor, I will take the unusual step of interrupting my statement for the defence to examine the woman Eucharis. I am told she is present here."

The Judge nodded his agreement, and after a brief consultation with Marcus Scaurus, Messalla reluctantly agreed, knowing that any objection from him would be badly interpreted by the court.

A richly but discreetly dressed Eucharis approached the court benches. Two men in particular watched her intensely. Marcus Scaurus realised that she would be forced to confirm his son's visit, but he calculated dispassionately that her greed for profiting from Helvia's conviction would keep her from making any other admissions which could weaken the prosecution. He had himself given the dice-box to Eucharis years ago, in more affluent days. Whatever reason she could adduce for giving it to his son would look bad. He would get the truth out of her on his next visit. Fufidius, on the other hand, was appalled, as he gazed at her. He did not believe she was involved in the crime, but he understood Cicero's tactics. Undoubtedly she was going to be used—quite ruthlessly—to help the defence. With the production of those few outrageous lines of poetry, the firm foundations of his family life had shivered for an instant—still shivered, even while his mind cried out "Slander!" And now Eucharis was under attack . . .

In reply to Cicero's questions, Eucharis denied any part in the young man's death. She knew him only as one who had attended her poetry salons a few times.

"And you told nobody of his visit to you the day of the Fufidii banquet, his last day of life?"

"No, I did not realise its significance."

"But you were curious and concerned enough to attend this trial, and you listened to the prosecutor emphasise how important it was to his case that Lucius Scaurus had no outside contacts that day?"

"I am a simple woman and do not understand such complicated matters." Eucharis cast down her eyes.

"You were educated by Parthenios? You read Greek drama? You copy Latin poems? And yet you did not understand the significance of that visit of Lucius Scaurus?"

"You confuse me," declared Eucharis. But her expression was anything but confused.

Cicero then asked her why she had given Lucius Scaurus a different wine from that which she had offered to Bibaculus. This, she said, was simply because Bibaculus had been drinking an everyday wine from the nearby Alban hills, but for a visitor from an important family like the Scauri she wished to offer a special wine. This was one from the slopes of Vesuvius, of which she had just received a consignment. And after drinking Alban wine, the palate of Bibaculus would not appreciate the Vesuvian wine.

"I see your experience in pleasing men," remarked Cicero in sarcastic tones. "And the dice-box, the jewelled dice-box? What do you say of that?"

Eucharis cast down her eyes again and hesitated.

"It was yours," pursued Cicero, "and yet you gave it to Lucius Scaurus. Why? What need had you to reward this young man?"

"Lucius Scaurus took the jewelled dice-box with him," agreed Eucharis. She paused, looked up at Cicero calmly and continued. "He took it because it was his and he had brought it with him." She paused again, and then said, "I refused to accept it as a present. Had I done so, Lucius Scaurus would have expected to come to me after the banquet, filled with wine and amorous—as all young men are—to claim my services."

A collective sigh of admiration came from most parts of the listening crowd as Eucharis retired from the witness stand. How cleverly she had turned Cicero's argument! She might even be telling the truth.

Young Quintus' neck and shoulders were taut to the point of agony as he watched Cicero smile, swing round at this juncture and walk away, his back to the jurors, playing almost the co-quette. Then suddenly he turned back, his handsome face intent as he set about demolishing whatever reputation Eucharis might have.

"Gentlemen, you have heard the testimony of the woman—this *learned* woman who is, at the same time and according to her own words, 'simple and confused'. Who could believe that rig-marole of hers which would have a penniless young man able to offer a most expensive present to a young Greek woman who, even more incredibly, then refuses it! Just think, if the dice-box had been his, and if he had sold it, he could have had the ser-vices of twenty young girls. If girls were his choice! No, it was hers and she was *obliged* to give it to him. The explanation is apparent. This Eucharis, whose unconvincing testimony you have just heard, must have been paying for his silence regarding some disreputable aspect of her life, past—or even present. I could hazard a guess about the present! You have heard her testimony. You have heard the words, 'filled with wine and amo-rous—as young men are—to claim my services'.

"As all young men are . . . indeed, we will believe her, and we may be sure enough, I think, that such services are not 'claimed' in vain. Such services are also not usually available without recompense. . . . It is all too easy for her to add to her profits from publishing. All young men are amorous—most will pay. I think it is very easy to imagine the sort of thing that

Eucharis would wish to remain secret—certainly from her patron! Her patron Fufidius, the husband of Helvia.

"Think how consistent this is with the whole character of Eucharis, from whom no word of that vitally important visit of Lucius Scaurus came until she was confronted with incontrovertible proof that it did take place. And you will have noted that not one word came voluntarily from her as to the purpose of his visit. This is not to be wondered at. Admission of the payment of blackmail would lead to other embarrassing questions and no other explanation has been forthcoming."

Cicero's words continued in grave and measured cadence.

"I will describe the background of this woman. Taken as a slave, this young and educated Greek was bought by the Fufidii, given duties of high responsibility as nurse to their children. Well treated, she yet behaved in such a way that Helvia was forced to send her away. She abandoned her next place of work, and being attractive and clever, she had little difficulty in providing entertainment to Roman men. She is not only *scholarly,* but she is an *artist* as well. She found work as a mime actress." Cicero paused. "A mime actress," he repeated, and his words lashed Eucharis now. "We have all of us seen mimes. We all know the type of woman who plays in them. All of us have breathed the hot, perfumed air of the stage, laughed at the crude plots, cheered at the rough jokes, clapped as the mime actress strips to the blare of trumpets. Only women of a certain sort have ever played *there.*"

Eucharis remained impassive.

"Even then," Cicero continued, "the family of the Fufidii were good to her. Fufidius bought her manumission, helped set her up in a house together with a son whom she produced without ever naming the father. What an object lesson in how to get on in the world. A girl of the mimes, now become respectable and even a successful businesswoman and a hostess of poetry salons. And now we may be sure that Fufidius expected from her a change of habits. He expected of her a private life befitting a freedwoman who seeks to establish herself in a respectable position.

"What did Lucius know of Eucharis? Enough for her to have been blackmailed into giving valuable 'presents' to him. To Lucius Scaurus, about to marry the daughter of her former mistress Helvia, who sent her away from the family home. To this day Eucharis hates Helvia for sending her away. Helvia could do nothing else because of Eucharis' misbehaviour, and she found Eucharis work elsewhere. Yet Eucharis hates. We all know the mentality of the ungrateful slave; and of all the slaves whom the gods see fit to provide us with, there is none so vindictive as the Greek.

"Imagine Eucharis' spiteful envy and anger when she learns that the daughter of the hated Helvia is to marry the son of the illustrious Marcus Aemilius Scaurus, and that with the dowry coming largely from her extensive estates, Helvia can ensure that the young man and his wife will enjoy a life forever denied to the son of a Eucharis—the illegitimate offspring of a slave. . . .

"So there we have it. Motive is there—in Eucharis' hatred of the woman who sent her away, in her envy of what Helvia could help to provide for a young man to whom she, Eucharis, seems now to have been blackmailed into giving valuable 'presents.' Opportunity—Lucius Scaurus' visit, which Eucharis expected, because she had a precious object ready to give to him. And a visit which she must never have expected to come to light because she knew that the only other person who knew of it would start the next day on a journey taking him far from Rome. And the banquet—the perfect opportunity to place the guilt on Helvia, just as the deceived family of Marcus Scaurus have tried to do. The means—the wine, a special wine indeed which the woman did not allow her other visitor to drink, and moreover a wine whose strong flavour, a unique flavour coming from the sulphurous soils of its origin, is well calculated to mask any trace of poison. A most respectable and observant lady present at the banquet, indeed, spoke at the time of the pallor of young Lucius Scaurus when he arrived.

"After all this, can you any longer take seriously the murder charge levelled at Helvia?

"But wait! There remains the absurd allegation of incest between Helvia and her brother to be disposed of. Were not the charge so serious, we would have to laugh at the so-called evidence. Look again, *iudices,* at the poem *Ad Helviam,* supposedly

written by Cinna. There are amongst you many men of culture,
with sound knowledge of literature. Could the poor author of
those limp lines really have thought they could plausibly be
ascribed to the greatest poet of our age? Why, even the metre is
deficient, the basic laws of poetry flouted. No, gentlemen, the
writer—none of us men of learning could call him poet—was
assuredly not Gaius Helvius Cinna.

"But this is a court of law, not a cultural discussion group. I
ask who provided this manuscript to the prosecutor. Can he produce a man—or a woman—who can stand here on the witness
bench and say, 'I stole this manuscript from Helvia?' For from
Helvia it would have had to come. And obviously not with her
consent. If such a man—or woman—can be shown to me, why
then I must acknowledge the authenticity of the poem, whatever
its technical deficiencies, and all that this authenticity would imply. But if such a man—or woman—otherwise reputable, cannot
be shown me, I am justified in branding the manuscript a scurri-
lous forgery, devoid of truth."

The silence was absolute. All knew this was the turning point.
Cicero gazed at the bench where all the Scaurus family sat. He
saw Marcus Scaurus and his *patronus* conferring with heads close
together. Cicero held his breath. He was gambling, but he could
swear that he had assessed the underlying situation. If the poem
was genuine, it was virtually certain that Eucharis had been the
thief, the theft dating from the time when she had been a personal slave of Helvia's. She would probably have stolen it to use
as a last resort if her situation should become desperate—or to
use to obtain wealth. She could have furnished it to the Scauri in
return for a rich reward if it helped to prove their charge against
Helvia. But now that Cicero had shown Eucharis to be little
more than a prostitute and one with motive and opportunity for
committing the murder, the prosecution could no longer afford
to put her forward as the supplier of the poem. Her story, true as
it might be, would not be believed now.

From the prosecution benches Marcus Valerius Messalla
slowly shook his head in answer to Cicero. Cicero relaxed.

"Gentlemen," he said. "We are entitled to conclude that the
poem is a forgery and that its imputation is entirely without
credibility. It was a pathetic attempt to destroy the deservedly

impeccable reputations of Helvia, wife to Fufidius, and of Cinna, poet and Tribune of the *plebs*.

"Now I have only one more question, gentlemen. What kind of man—or woman—is best placed to have a slanderous poem composed by a practising poet and written by a professional scribe? Would it not be a man—or a woman—already active in publishing poems?"

Cicero sat down amidst total silence. He had destroyed the prosecution case and the judges and the audience all knew it.

Witnesses were called to give evidence. Messalla might wax very sarcastic and insinuating about Fufidius' refusal to have his slaves interrogated under torture concerning the evidence of magic in his garden. He might use every trick in his repertoire to shake the confidence of Fufidius' freedman concerning this. To no avail. In the altercation that followed Cicero was biting and wholly effective. The acquittal was inevitable.

XXIV

Extravagantly praised and viciously abused for so many hours past, Helvia fell thankfully into the arms of her family after the acquittal. Friends and well-wishers engulfed them. Bewildered, half fainting, she hardly understood the case was won and her only thought was to escape from the eyes of the public. Between Fufidius and her son, she was finally borne away, though no one wanted to let her go.

She was stumbling down the steep steps of the Basilica when, in all the pandemonium, she became aware of a presence at the bottom and saw Marcus Scaurus' staring hard eyes and his white face. He stood rock-still and their eyes met. Helvia saw his lips move in a curse and she trembled as Fufidius hurried her through the crush to where the slaves waited with her carriage.

Relief from pressure was long in coming. She would wake in the grip of dread of a coming trial and would once more wearily try to grasp the reality that it was past. Perhaps the nightmare would never end. Pressures had shifted, that was all. The very quality of life had changed. Not only she, but those dearest and closest had been dragged into the open and their private lives mauled over in public debate. They had won their case, but accusations had been made, and no matter if true or false, the damage had been done. All these confused strands made up her troubled dreams.

"I want the truth this time."

Marcus Scaurus was not long in confronting a trembling Eucharis. She had spent a wretched night. She had put in Scaurus' hands what she thought was a sure weapon. She had laid plans; and she had calculated wrongly. Cicero had destroyed her so easily in court. His eloquence and wit had crushed her. She had felt his dislike of her, so strong, behind the biting phrases. This had unnerved her. Men usually liked her.

She did her best now with Scaurus. She had put perfume on; she had combed her hair. She looked up at him, looked down, and murmured, "I did it for you, only for you. I wanted Helvia to pay for what she did to you." She made her lips tremble and her eyes well.

Scaurus' hands dug into her soft arms and he forced her gaze. "Who wrote the incest poem? Was it you yourself or did you get one of those paid poets to do it?"

"It was the brother of Helvia, and no one else!" she protested.

He knew her for an accomplished and charming liar, but he thought that this was probably true. "Cicero said the metre was faulty. You say you know about such things . . ."

"It was not bad verse," she asserted. "There was a slip or two, but perhaps it had been hastily written. Cinna is a master. It was done a long time ago, when he was young."

"Well, I'm not up in these things," said Scaurus awkwardly. "I'm no judge of poetry."

"Most of the judges were not either. Cinna writes for other poets. He says that Cicero writes poetry that is metrically perfect, but all the same is no poet. But few understand such niceties. Cicero has a reputation as a poet, and no one in court could argue with him."

Scaurus scowled. He had, quite unfairly, taunted his leading counsel with having been unable to argue—extempore—the merits of that poem.

"You didn't tell me Lucius visited you here the day of his death."

"There was no reason to tell you. I did think Furius Bibaculus was safely in Africa," she asserted bravely.

"Why did Lucius come?"

She had anticipated this. She had best be economical with the truth. "He wanted a loan."

"The dice-box, then . . ."

"I gave it to him," she admitted. "At the time I had little money actually in the house." She added desperately, "Please, I beg you, don't reveal our relationship to Fufidius. He has done so much for me."

Scaurus cut through her words relentlessly. "What about that other poem, the one Lucius was said to have read out here, at one of your gatherings?" Scaurus' face was very angry. "Give it to me," he ordered. "I can tell there was such a poem by the way Gellius and Metellus were sniggering away on their jury benches."

Terrified now, Eucharis went out of the room and came back with a little roll. There was complete silence while Scaurus unrolled the paper and narrowed his eyes over it. Then he said, "I can't make it all out. My eyes aren't good now. You read it." He added, "It's no use trying to trick me. I *can* read it, only it strains my eyes."

Submissively, she read it aloud for him. It sounded terrible in her mouth, at this time.

Scaurus groaned. "Lucius read that out? To whom?"

"He was very drunk," she said gently. "He did not know what he said." She told him who had been present.

Only that morning Scaurus had had a fearful row with his young relative Decimus Scaurus who, tired of being assailed for his lack of culture in the matter of poetry, had spitefully mentioned that the poem was "in great demand about town."

"Lucius Aemilius Scaurus—the first letters of each line even spelling out his name . . . and this is going the rounds now?" Marcus Scaurus swore, long and bitterly, as he sat there. "And I need hardly ask," he sneered, "whose composition *this* was!"

"Of course it was Cinna's, Cinna's," she cried. "Just as the other was."

"I suppose," he said grudgingly, "I have to believe that you had no hand in the incest poem."

"Oh," she cried despairingly, "you surely *can't* believe what Cicero said. Everything I have told you is true. Everything. How could I possibly have arranged for these poems to be written? Who would have done *my* bidding? Oh, what is to become of me now? After Cicero has accused me of the murder of your son!"

"You?" She had hardly entered into his consideration. "Nothing . . . You've been too clever, Eucharis. You've played a dangerous game with everyone, me included. If I thought you had put poison in Lucius' wine when he was here just before the banquet, or if I thought you *had* written the poem, I would strangle you here and now and enjoy doing it." He looked at her dispassionately. "And no one would care a damn."

He got up and stood over her, then his hands closed round her neck and began to squeeze.

"Just a little more pressure, Eucharis, and you would be dead."

His hands travelled down her body in an embrace half savage, half sensual. Then he thrust her away and strode out of the apartment. His litter-bearers forced their way through the tortuous alleys of the Subura, crammed with stalls and shops. Somewhere metal clanged on metal. Men shoved and rough voices shouted. Scaurus hardly noticed, though the noise was deafening. His son, who had been his pride, done to death by that unclean pair Cinna and his sister Helvia. And he had been ridiculed before his inferiors as well. A letter had reached him from his elder son in Spain. He had survived the battle of Munda and was still with his stepbrother Sextus Pompeius, the only leader to escape death. "I have dreadful reports of Lucius' behaviour at Thapsus from Sextus. No doubt Lucius is keeping safe in Rome by now . . ."

Had Lucius deserted? Whether it was true or not, Cinna had got hold of a story and made a fool of Lucius when the boy was drunk. He had insulted him before a gathering of sniggering poets. Following that, he or his precious sister had poisoned him. Scaurus was absolutely sure of this. The pair thought they had won. Scaurus had failed to expose Helvia. Cinna was Tribune now, his person sacrosanct. For the time being . . . But sacrosanct or not, Tribune or not, there would be no mistake next time. . . .

Cinna visited Helvia whenever he could get away from the Forum—but never were they alone together now. And he was preoccupied with his official duties as Tribune.

Spring—uneasy, fitful and often violent—had come early that year of 44 B.C. Flowers already blossomed in the fields and along the verges of the great consular roads, while market stalls in the streets leading to the Forum became patches of colour against the brick and stone of the city.

Caesar worked furiously for the betterment of Rome and its

people. But since mid-February he had become dictator for life. *Dictator perpetuus.* King in all but name. Oh, the title "Rex" he had refused most vehemently and in public, but he wore the high red boots of the ancient kings and was draped in their purple, sitting on his golden throne. Where was the republic now? The senators, feeling themselves men of clay now, mere ciphers, outdid each other in heaping insulting honours on his head.

"Their provocation knows no bounds," said Cinna bitterly, one afternoon when he sat with Helvia in her garden. Fufidia was there as well—a forlorn little figure nowadays.

The sun blazed sudden and hot on their backs. From above the tremulous green newness of leaf and the filmy blossom of an early apple tree cast smudgy patterns. Slaves came and went.

"They'll vote him anything," Cinna went on. " 'Jupiter Julius' is his latest title; and a temple consecrated to him, with Marcus Antonius his priest!"

He talked endlessly and worriedly of the battle he continually had with other Tribunes, who were protesting that they could not speak their minds any longer on behalf of the people. Cinna owed his advancement to Caesar, but it dragged heavy on him now.

To Helvia it meant little. She was listless and idle now. She only prayed for Cinna's success and safety. She had never wanted him to be Tribune. She wished him out of it all, leading a leisured, well-to-do life. Wasn't his poetry enough? That would endure.

Outside in the streets, the whole city shuddered as reports of strange signs and apparitions passed from mouth to mouth. By night, lights in the sky and crashing sounds, a great crowd of men charging, all on fire. Caesar's life was threatened, it was clear. At Capua, colonisers breaking up some ancient tombs for stone turned up a bronze tablet warning that a man of Trojan stock would be murdered by his kindred. A herd of horses dedicated by Caesar to the Rubicon were weeping and refusing to eat. During a sacrifice, an augur warned Caesar of the Ides of March . . .

Some days later, Cinna came again to see Helvia. He was nervous, flushed, and his throat, he said, was dry. He drank a great deal of water, then some wine. Before he left, Helvia took his hands, "Gaius, you are not well. Your hands are hot." She felt his forehead. It was burning.

"Perhaps I have a little fever." He smiled at her. "More than anything, I'm depressed. I'd like to get away from Rome, far away from the accursed Forum." He was silent a moment and then burst out, "The Senate, fawning, spitting, hostile, impotent, *obsolete;* a hated Caesar, overriding them all, in his frenzy to get things done—as though he hasn't much time. And *how* he is hated. Oh, stand off and look at the state of the world. . . ."

Helvia looked at him uncomprehending as Cinna moved restlessly. "A strange thing happened yesterday," he went on. "A little wren flew into the Senate meeting with a sprig of laurel in its beak. Then a swarm of big birds after it. They tore the wren to pieces."

Helvia shivered and pressed closer to him.

"The worst of all," Cinna dropped his voice to a whisper, "is that I can't make love to you."

Before he left he produced a fat roll of manuscript. "Here are various bits and pieces. *You* take them."

"Why, Gaius . . ." she exclaimed in surprise.

"I'd like you to have them."

Disregarding anyone who was near, he grasped her shoulders and kissed her hungrily, rather desperately. Then he stroked her cheek. "Helvia, my dear dear Helvia, be of good heart," he whispered. Then he clasped Fufidia to him tenderly. In an instant he was gone.

That was the fourteenth day of March.

The next day, on the Ides of March, Caesar was assassinated.

XXV

Towards dusk, Fufidius brought news home. Helvia leapt up, wild with fear. She had one thought. "Oh, have you seen Gaius? Is he all right? Tell me, have you seen him?" she sobbed.

"All is well with your brother. He wasn't even at the meeting of the Senate. He's at home with a fever. I've seen him. I passed by his house," Fufidius told her.

Helvia sank down on a chair, not able to stop trembling, even laughing now, in nervousness. "I am stupid."

Fufidius gazed at her in dismay. Behind the news of Caesar's death, his mind groped at the question which ran now like a rotten seam through his steadfast devotion to his family. Were she and Cinna really lovers? At that moment he could swear from her expression that the answer was yes . . . Shutting the thought from his mind, Fufidius launched into an account of what he knew of the day's happenings, the true and false of which were spreading like a fire through the City.

"They killed him in the annex to Pompeius' theatre, where the Senate was assembled today. He fell at the base of Pompeius' statue. It was all planned. One after another the conspirators stabbed him. Twenty-three blows in all, they say. The pedestal of the statue is drenched in blood. The whole Senate has fled. All the shops are shut and people have done little but rush to look, then rush back home again and stay there."

The conspirators had installed themselves on the Capitol. Cicero had advised them to summon the Senate to the Temple of Jupiter.

News trickled in—of senators locked in their houses, too terrified to come out, of Caesar lying dead for long hours where he had been struck down, no one daring to approach the blood-stained corpse.

Next day, Caesar's will was unsealed and read in Antonius' house. Caesar had left his gardens on the Tiber's bank to the people, and three gold pieces to each man. And now rumblings of anger were sounding in all Rome, welling up from the masses below.

Helvia's family gathered round her. She had been distraught at Cinna having thrust on her that sheaf of poems. Had he a premonition? At her bidding, Fufidius himself went early once more to Cinna's house. He came back to say Cinna felt better but was still weak. He had promised he would not attend Caesar's funeral. Cinna had had a dream, he said. He had dreamed that Caesar invited him to supper and he declined. Caesar then led him along by the hand, though Cinna did not want to go and was pulling away . . . At all events, Helvia must not worry. He would stay in bed at home.

Helvia cried for relief. At last she found rest and slept long and heavily all that day.

Cinna, lying at home, could not rid himself of that dream. Caesar had been his good friend. The dream probably meant that he should attend his funeral. He rose. He felt better, only dizzy. He drank a little water, and had his slaves arrange his toga about him. His slaves protested, his head freedman also. Curtly, Cinna told them he would go out. And he did not want their whining presence with him, nor his bearers. He would go alone. It was only a short distance to the Forum. Forthwith he left the house.

But though he did not know it, he did not go alone. There was a shadow, which had followed Cinna for days past. The shadow materialised from nowhere, there in the street . . .

Down in the Forum Marcus Antonius, who had been Caesar's right-hand man, forthright and open, and never more masculine, never more appealing, declaimed over Caesar's dead body. Cinna pushed his way through the jostling, excited multitude.

"Anger did not brutalise Caesar," Antonius' voice rang out with conviction, "nor good fortune corrupt him. Power did not alter him, nor authority change him. He has well been called the father of his country. Yet this father, this high priest, this inviolable being, this hero and god is dead. Dead, alas, not by the violence of disease, nor wasted by old age, nor wounded abroad in war, nor caught up by some supernatural force, but dead within the walls of Rome. This man, who safely led an army into Britain, has been cut down in the city; this man, bravest of warriors, has been killed while unarmed and defenceless. This man, whom no enemy succeeded in killing, has been done to death by his comrades to whom he so often showed mercy.

"Of what avail your laws? You lie dead in the Forum through which you have so often led a triumph. Ah woe, for the blood-bespattered grey locks, alas for the torn robe, which you assumed, it seems, only that you might be slain in it—"

At this the throng, excited and inflamed, rushed to seize Caesar's body. They wanted to burn it in the place where he had been slaughtered. But the soldiers, fearing for the theatre and temples, fought them off and placed Caesar's body upon a pyre there in the Forum.

The tumultuous scene swam before Cinna's eyes. All about him men cursed and threatened death to the conspirators. In the grip of mass hysteria and rage, they were capable of anything. The gruesome faces bewildered him, the bestial roars deafened him. Weak and dizzy, his body had turned to water.

Close by, someone called his name. "Cinna! Cinna!"

He turned. "Who calls me? I am Cinna."

A man shouted. "It's Cinna! One of the conspirators!"

Then a private furor struck those immediately around him. "Cinna! Cinna!" rose the shout. Someone laid hold of him. "Cornelius Cinna! One of the murderers of our great Caesar. Kill him! Kill!"

"I am not the Praetor Cornelius Cinna! I am Gaius *Helvius* Cinna!" he cried frantically, but his cry was lost in the roaring, collective blood lust of the crowd.

"Cinna, Cinna, kill him! Kill him!" The chant gathered volume, enveloping all.

A crazed and brutal face closed on him. Hands went around Cinna's throat, throttling out the life. Frenzied in their hatred, the crowd knew no mercy. They tore at his limbs.

"Get back, get back, let me at him," shouted someone. "We'll have his head . . ."

And a short sword swished down viciously over the broken body.

Money changed hands that night. Much money. From Marcus Scaurus to that client of his who had shadowed Cinna for so many days with instructions to await his chance. Caesar's funeral, the frenzy of the crowd, had given him the opportunity. Before then it had been impossible. Cinna, inviolate as Tribune, was always surrounded by a crowd of slaves, henchmen, clients, claimants of some sort on his time. And when not so surrounded, then in that litter of his, with those enormous brown bearers. Always there had been witnesses.

Today had come the reward for his unremitting vigilance. A Cinna alone, in a crowd, a Cinna sick and weak moreover. And what a crowd, what savagery ready to be aroused and used. All that was needed was to cry out his name and then, when he answered, to name him the conspirator Cornelius Cinna. And to leave the rest to the inflamed mob. . . .

"You have done well, Spurius Rustius," Marcus Scaurus told his henchman. "The thing was most dexterously done. I will see that you go far, for you have saved the honour of our family. That this murdering hypocrite of a poet should not only have been killed but, ah, that his head should have been put on a pole and carried aloft by the crowd was something I would never had dared hope for."

Exultant, Marcus Scaurus clasped his man warmly by the shoulders.

Fufidius, returning home that night, put his head in his hands and cried like a child.

"O gods above, help me," he sobbed. "How can I ever tell Helvia? How can I ever tell her?"

XXVI

Life in Rome was in turmoil following the assassination of Caesar. He had bestridden the world and now no man felt his own life unaffected. Mobs gathered to hurl threats of reprisal and vengeance against the assassins. The funeral oration of Marcus Antonius inflamed people even more. Senators not usually noted for timidity stayed home behind locked doors. The city again resounded to the sound of marching as Antonius gathered troops from Latium. Rumours sped from the most diverse sources, from salons, baths and market places. Older people spoke darkly of the portentous blaze of a comet which had streaked across the sky for seven nights after Caesar's death. The sun's orb rose dim and pale, its heat feeble and ineffectual. Vapours lay dark and heavy on the earth, and fruit and vegetables did not properly ripen. The divine power or genius which had been Caesar's during life remained active now, to avenge his death.

Caesar had become dictator for life and this was more than proud aristocrats could bear. Kill the tyrant they must—a noble act—but what, or who, could take his place? The Senate's rigid and creaking machinery, unchanging since time out of mind, had long been ineffectual. All trembled.

In all this confusion, Marcus Scaurus continued to exult over the death of Cinna, and his clan with him. A debt had been paid in full. A life had been paid with a life. But it was to be their last burst of activity, a symbolic death frenzy of the family itself, bringing no gain but the salty taste of vengeance. For the Scauri, that spring heralded only a continuing decline. The loss of the expected dowry, which would have benefited the family as well as the son himself, compounded by the costs of the trial. High public office with the opportunity to plunder revenues did not come their way again. Lucius' elder brother was later to betray his own stepbrother Sextus Pompeius to Marcus Antonius. The

family returned to the obscurity from which the energy and hard
work of earlier generations had lifted it.

For the Fufidii, the sweetness of relief after the trial was followed too quickly by the thunderbolt of Cinna's death. Helvia
went almost mad with grief. The woman whom her household
was accustomed to see in full control of all their lives was trans-
formed into a semi-recluse. Her life turned inwards. The two
children were her only comfort. Gratidia, in her self-effacing
way, contributed a sorely needed normality.

Public disorder forced Fufidius to go about his affairs as quietly as possible. Marcus Antonius held the centre of the stage
now, but in April Gaius Octavius, the young boy whom Caesar
had named his heir, arrived in Rome. No one knew what would
happen, but between this polite, cold youth of eighteen years
and the big, bluff and brilliant general Antonius, Consul and
now head of the government, trouble could be anticipated. Further power struggles were certain, further fighting of Roman
against Roman, with all that might ensue in the way of confisca-
tions and arbitrary taxation. Fufidius transferred from Rome
much of the cash he had accumulated for the payment of his
daughter's dowry and hid it away in his more secluded Arpinate
and Tusculum villas.

It was Fufidius' private world which was so difficult to rebuild.
Threatened first by Helvia's being charged with poisoning, the
spectre of her alleged incest threatened to destroy that world's
shaken remains. To ensure Helvia's acquittal, Cicero had destroyed Eucharis' character in court. Fufidius' faith in her had
trembled. He suffered, for in Eucharis he had invested money;
on her account had known jealousy. She owed him loyalty, not
only gratification.

Murder. To his last days, Fufidius did not know who had killed
Lucius Scaurus. He acknowledged that Eucharis had had the opportunity but thought Cicero's implication of her no more than a
clever tactic. He thought of his son's evident and burning hatred
of Lucius. He thought of Cinna . . . then of Helvia and Cinna.
The intensity of Helvia's grief at Cinna's death made him think
the worst. But he shrank from asking her.

Fufidius went to Eucharis. He asked her about the poem *Ad
Helviam*. She fell at his feet and swore she knew nothing of the

poem. She did not know how Scaurus had got hold of it. She had
never looked more beseeching, sweeter. They settled down to
discuss who might have written it. Eucharis told him of Lucius'
drunkenness the evening of the Saturnalia celebrations at her
house. If Lucius had afterwards realised just what he had read—
and nothing, Eucharis declared, was more sure than that some
kind friend would tell him—he would not have let the insult pass
without counterattack. And what better riposte than an answer-
ing poem? A poem asserting that Cinna's private life was even
worse. Lucius had been the darling of so many men—
Parthenios, for instance, had been most attentive to him that
night. A Parthenios could certainly have written *Ad Helviam!*

Fufidius jumped at that. Parthenios, indeed! Just the sort. . . .
No, no, Eucharis hastened to say, she only gave him as an example. She knew Parthenios better than most. He had been her
benefactor as a child. Fufidius must promise—Eucharis pouted
here, disarmingly—that he would not attack Parthenios. The
thing was that Lucius could easily have persuaded one of his
lovers to write such a poem.

"You are a very clever young woman, *voluptas mea,"* breathed
Fufidius. "And lovelier than ever as the days pass. . . ."

The more he thought the more convinced he was she was
right.

Eucharis looked up at him with her dark limpid eyes and put a
gentle hand on him. "O-o-oh," she sobbed, and pulled him to
her.

"You are right," he breathed in her ear. "That is how it happened. . . ."

"And then Lucius' father found the poem," she whispered,
rather indistinctly, as her hands explored him.

"Oh, poor brave Eucharis," thought Fufidius. How badly she
had been used at the trial. Cicero had had to be formally
thanked, but how unjustly he had blackened her character. Perhaps she should have come forward to disclose Lucius' visit the
morning of the banquet because it was so important for the defence of Helvia. But with her hard experience of life in Rome—
and how difficult it was for a girl slave to make her way honestly
in that life—surely she was to be pardoned for not having done

so. Look how Cicero had tried to discredit her transparently truthful account of that dice-box!

At home, tossing wakeful through the sweet-scented spring nights, Fufidius thought of his children. Such good, loving children. "Let things rest, Fufidius," he would nightly decide, in the small hours. "Enough harm has been done. Let things rest now, for their sake."

So, one night at dinner, with friends and relatives present and with a large number of servants waiting on them, Fufidius said, "I am proud of you, children. It has been a dreadful time. But you have been as good and brave as anyone could wish. The charges that Marcus Scaurus brought against your mother and his other allegations were incredible. Grief must have sent him mad." He looked at Helvia squarely then, then at the others. "All lies," he said, "dreadful lies."

They murmured concurrence.

Fufidius continued. "One positive thing the trial did was to establish our boy Quintus as a pleader of merit. Mind you, my son, you had only to tell the truth, in your mother's case."

He embraced Helvia, and then his children. Fufidius had made up his mind and taken his stand. This firm decision on loyalties was invigorating. Before long Eucharis asked Fufidius for more help for little Pamphilus. Fufidius told her he would give the boy his freedom as soon as the troubled times allowed.

"He will be educated," he told her, "and then he will work for me. In the years to come, I shall need an assistant. Quintus will make his way as an advocate and gain important public office, but I want someone working closely with me whom I can trust to manage my estates and help with my loans."

Eucharis was happy now. She might even renew her efforts to have Fufidius adopt Pamphilus. But it could come later . . .

Some weeks afterwards, Fufidius completed arrangements for his family to remove to the villa by the sea in Herculaneum. It was still spring rather than summer, but he could see that they would all benefit by moving away from Rome and their recent troubled lives. Young Quintus needed a break from his studies, while Helvia and Fufidia might well make the acquaintance there of a family with a son who was ready for marriage. Fufidius knew the social function of resorts like Herculaneum and this was a place where you would find only the best of families. He hoped that Helvia, now regaining some of her usual vigour, would not be tempted again into that ridiculous Isis sect which flourished down in those parts. But he was sure that she had learned her lesson. The house in Rome could be closed. He himself proposed to go to Gaul again on business as soon as it was safe to travel there. In the meantime he could see more of Eucharis and perhaps expand the publishing business further.

By the end of May, therefore, Gratidia who was unwilling to face the long journey to Herculaneum was installed with several of her old friends in the villa at Tusculum. One afternoon she had the gratification of a message from Cicero to say that he proposed to visit her the following day. Great man that he was, he had always found time to talk with his elderly and distant kinswoman. In the past his daughter had often accompanied him on these visits, and like the Fufidii family, had called her Aunt Gratidia. "Poor Tullia," she thought. She had died tragically young.

Gratidia received him in the terraced garden, the very same which had seen Fufidia's first meeting with Lucius Scaurus. Already the smell of another summer was in the air, with its lazy sensual invitation.

"You are good to visit an old woman." Gratidia had made herself up carefully for the occasion, the flickering light through the vines striking her various jewelled neckbands firm around her thick neck, her still handsome brown eyes sparkling from her lined face. She settled herself fussily on her couch and kept smoothing her robe as they chatted.

"What times we live in. I am glad you escape to this quiet place for a little."

She thought Cicero looked very tired, not from healthy exertion, but nervously tired from inactivity and depression. He was jumpy rather than vivacious. But the famous man did not mind bathing in the admiration of his old relative and confiding in her a little. She was a safe repository in her age and isolation from affairs.

"Tell me," she questioned him, "your views on the assassination."

"You ask *me* that? A glorious act, but incomplete!" he spoke in Greek, his eyes sliding to the servants within earshot.

Gratidia waved the slaves away. "Incomplete?" she faltered.

"Oh, Marcus Antonius should have gone too. You see, the tyranny has survived the tyrant." Cicero's eyes moved restlessly.

"So!" Gratidia, delighted and fearful to hear him talk so openly, gripped the arms of her chair, her eyes glued to his face.

"And now Caesar's adopted son has come to claim his inheritance. Antonius is sitting on it, and on all the money left by Caesar."

"The young man is from Velitrae, I know."

"Yes, a clever boy, very clever. Eighteen. Slight and delicate in health. His own men call him Caesar. *I* did not. He is very polite to *me.* I see a future for him. I could use Octavius."

Gratidia's face twitched with satisfaction. She leaned forward, her hands fondling each other with pleasure. "They all want *your* advice, and *your* experience. Cinna told me Caesar wanted you, Pompeius too." She took a great breath and held it, as if to savour his great wisdom as a perfume. Cicero waved a modestly disclaiming hand and smiled.

They talked for a little about Octavius, Cicero making her laugh with his barbed jokes about the youth. "Let us gossip of more intimate things," he said. "Even now, I'm still not sure what happened in the death of Lucius Scaurus." He paused. "Helvia?" After a moment he added, "The more I think of it, the more sure I am."

Gratidia raised her eyebrows, but said nothing. He smiled coaxingly at her.

"You understand, Gratidia, that any intelligent assessment of the evidence points most strongly indeed to her. Precisely as the prosecutor for the Scauri said. Helvia hated the young man. The magic showed that conclusively. And undoubtedly the poison was administered at the banquet. Despite your brave attempt, Gratidia, to suggest that Scaurus was already pale when he arrived there."

"Oh, but you must believe me . . ." she began. "I looked at him very closely that night . . ."

Cicero held up a mocking hand. "Yes, yes . . ."

She, who would give way to few, did so to him.

"If Lucius was pale," Cicero continued, "it had nothing to do with visiting Eucharis. She is a liar of course. Greeks have never understood the significance of a solemn oath in a court of law. And it is quite clear that she was being blackmailed by Lucius Scaurus, whatever the reason. The dice-box!" He laughed. "She was very clever in her reply. With those quick wits she would have made a good advocate herself. But one thing is certain. She was not so much of a fool as to administer poison in front of a witness. I mean Furius Bibaculus. There was too much chance he would turn up with his account of what happened there. As he did."

Cicero mused for a while on the problems he had faced in defending Helvia. "She took a big risk."

"Who did?"

"Why, Helvia, of course," he answered. "I suppose she never thought that the story of her relationship with her brother would come out. That really damned her."

"But the court did find her innocent of murder," observed Gratidia.

"Only because of my advocacy," he returned seriously. "Although I was sure she had poisoned him, that was no reason why she should be found guilty. After all, I have known the Fufidii for many years and from what I have heard of Lucius Scaurus, Helvia saved her daughter from a most unsuitable union. It was difficult for me, though. The only defence I could try was to show that someone else had at least equal opportunity and motive. The Greek woman Eucharis fitted my requirements perfectly. Fufidius will never forgive me, but there was no other way.

"That poem *Ad Helviam* which the prosecution sprang on me was a shock," he continued. "Fortunately, I guessed how they had got hold of it. While it could have been stolen by somebody else, Eucharis was the logical supplier. So once I had blackened the character of Eucharis, the prosecution could not acknowledge its authenticity." He thought again for a moment, and smiled. "Fortunate, too, that it was written when Cinna was still a very young poet and that the metre was uncertain. No one cared to argue this out with me."

"No, no," Gratidia hastened to say. "Famous as you are yourself as a poet!"

"The judges all like to think of themselves as men of culture, so none felt he could disagree with my assessment of it. I was very happy at the result." Cicero smiled complacently.

A little breeze rustled the rose leaves then, and there was a subtle change of air. Did Cinna's shade stir? Did Cinna's laughter echo faintly around the vine-covered terrace?

Gratidia sighed as she endeavoured to ease her rheumatism. She looked at Cicero's alert eyes that gazed at her so promptingly. She laughed then, uncertainly, thought one moment, then submitted.

"I am an old woman now," she began, "and can have only a few years left. There is no harm in telling you how it all happened. Helvia and Cinna were furious at Fufidius' marrying the daughter to Lucius Scaurus. I think Cinna was even more angry than Helvia because he adored his unacknowledged daughter, and to see another man arrange her marriage—even if he was Helvia's husband—was more than he could easily bear."

Cicero interrupted her. "So Cinna had the real feelings of a father? Well, I feel for him."

"He soon found out that Lucius Scaurus was exactly the type of man who would make the worst of husbands—arrogant, selfish, dissipated and unduly attracted to men. As you know, Cinna then manoeuvred Scaurus into reading out—in the company of a number of men—a poem which was a marvel of self-humiliation. He expected to provoke Lucius into retaliating. He thought Lucius would try to kill him then and there, and this would have been a crime, because Cinna was already Tribune. Then the marriage would have had to be broken off. Cinna thought Lucius was just drunk enough to do it. But in fact, Lucius was so drunk he did not understand properly what he was reading. The weaknesses of men at times become their good fortune." Gratidia's lips curled scornfully.

"So Lucius was left humiliated," Cicero commented.

In the caressing warmth of the summer afternoon Gratidia shivered a little. "Oh, but he got his revenge on our family, most horribly," she said slowly. "He had a group of his slaves seize

young Quintus and rape him. By chance I was there when they
dumped him back, broken in spirit and bloody in body."

The lovely blue of the sky and the bird song faded for Gratidia as in her mind's eye she saw once more her nephew Quintus crawl rather than walk into the house in Rome that winter
night. He had pulled himself onto a couch. Speechless for a
while, he had finally blurted the story out. From the afternoon's
Olympian dreams of his future brilliant life he had been taken
and whipped and forced to submit sexually to slaves. With the
confession, his will had broken and his youthfulness took over
and he had writhed on the floor weeping.

"Only that day you had given him his first lesson in public
speaking." Gratidia's voice quavered at the memory and her
eyes filled.

She had not said anything to Quintus, but gathered him into
her arms and cradled his head until his weeping ceased and he
grew calmer. She had helped him to the bathroom and the youth
became a child again for a time as she bathed him and applied
ointments and put a clean robe over his suffering body. She gave
him her special cakes to eat, sweetened with honey, and poured
a strong, sweet wine.

In the quietness of the room and the tenderness of the old
woman, so different from her usual fussy self, Quintus had gradually revived. His body still ached and throbbed, but it no
longer bled. And it had been cleaned.

"He made me promise," said Gratidia, "as he began to recover, he made me promise. He made me swear that his father
would never know of his shame. He said his father would be
forced to kill Lucius Scaurus. He said the whole family would be
ruined as a result."

Cicero got to his feet and strode up and down on the terrace.
"A distasteful tale." He turned suddenly to Gratidia. "And a
strong enough motive for killing Lucius Scaurus."

Gratidia shook her head. "Young Quintus did not kill him."

Cicero's eyes narrowed. "But you told Helvia."

"I have never told anyone, nor must you."

Cicero was silent, waiting. Gratidia looked very dreamy.

"Cinna found out?"

Gratidia raised her eyes to the roses overhead. "He had no hand in Lucius' death."

"You seem very sure, Gratidia. So sure who *did not* do it that I feel you must know who *did*. Was it someone outside the family —never suspected and paying off a grudge? Why, was it Eucharis after all?"

Gratidia looked at him straight now. "Not at all," she said. She paused and then went on calmly. "I killed him myself. I couldn't let Lucius marry Fufidia. It was all too likely that young Quintus would take his revenge, sooner or later. Who knows where it would all have ended? Lucius Scaurus was despicable. Cinna assured me that he did run away from Thapsus. Oh, poor Cinna," Gratidia faltered now. "Poor Cinna. I have often wondered if the Scauri did, after all, take their revenge on him at Caesar's funeral."

Cicero sat down suddenly. "Gratidia, this time you catch me completely by surprise," he admitted, gazing at his old relative. "So you felt you had to take matters into your own hands?"

"It was very simple," said the old woman modestly. "For years I had kept that poison in case my pains got too bad to be worth suffering. Nobody notices an old woman like me. I left early to go to bed. As I went, they were all standing up to watch the jugglers. It was easy to slip the powder in Lucius' goblet. It was aconite, a nicely measured dose prepared for me by an old doctor friend of mine many years dead now, guaranteed to produce death painlessly. But I expected Lucius' death only after several days and not that same night.

"I wrote a confession, with details, in case it was needed to protect Helvia. I have it still. And this helped to reassure Fufidia, who was terrified." Gratidia smiled disarmingly at Cicero. "But I knew that you would certainly demonstrate Helvia's innocence."

She paused reflectively.

"Helvia will never recover completely from losing Cinna," she continued. "But she has her children. She has Isis, too. You know it is a religion that suits us women."

Once more she fell silent, adding, after a minute, "Perhaps in his way Fufidius is the best of us all. He protects his wife, cares for his children, loves his woman and makes money. Perhaps," she added, "a touch of cynicism would help." Gratidia gave a little giggle. "And now, my dear Cicero, will you drink some wine with me?"

Cicero's body jerked. He laughed somewhat forcedly, and said, *"Bene, bene."*

He nodded his head and Gratidia clapped her hands for a slave to bring wine. Then she sent the slave away.

She arranged the glasses herself on a little tray and then Cicero, watching her, gave a somewhat sickly smile and said, "It took courage, what you did." His words almost embraced her. "You deserve this rest. This rest on a lovely terrace, the result of Fufidius' excellent business head and impeccable taste. Indeed. How many pretty things there are here! The little marble boy over there . . ." His eyes were on a statue slightly behind her. "Hermes. I think it is a modern copy, but a wonderful copy, of the Hermes of Praxiteles, isn't it?"

Laboriously, in her old woman's way, Gratidia shifted her body round to look at the statue. In that moment, very deftly, Cicero switched glasses. Gratidia turned again to face Cicero and they toasted the health of their respective families.

POSTSCRIPT

London, June 1988

Our knowledge of the later history of the Fufidii is scattered and sparse. For a time they disappeared from Rome, but it seems that they were back in Arpinum the following year—the year that saw the brutal murder of Cicero in the ruthless proscriptions of the triumvirs. In Arpinum, Fufidius made yet another contract of marriage for Fufidia, this time, it may be assumed, with the prior agreement of Helvia. It was with a young Arpinate of means and —most important—first cousin to the Marcus Vipsanius Agrippa who was such a friend of the future emperor Augustus. This was the same Agrippa who was to have a brilliant military career, attain the consulship and initiate many fine public buildings in Rome, not least the Pantheon, where his name still adorns the portico. His bust, together with that of Cicero and of Gaius Marius, graces the Piazza Municipio of Arpinum to this day. Such a connection must certainly have been enough to safeguard Fufidius from any danger of proscription.

It is reported that Fufidia's marriage was a most happy one, the husband being very satisfied indeed with his young wife, so beautiful and blond, and—unlike some women—quiet and submissive. And fertile—they had numerous sons.

Cicero's speech *Pro Helvia* was included amongst those prepared for publication by his secretary Tiro and is still read, though not usually as prescribed reading in the diminishing number of schools where Latin continues to be studied.

And that would be all, were it not for the following letter which came to light in damaged but decipherable condition in Herculaneum, that fashionable seaside resort of Roman days, in the course of excavations last year by a combined British/American archaeological team:

Scr. Arpini a.d. xiv Kal. Oct. 729 a.u.c.
(Arpinum, September 18, 25 B.C.)

From Fufidia to her darling brother Quintus, Greetings.

If only I could see you! I hope, however, that you will come to Arpinum after your respite from all the work involved in the important law cases you have taken on in Rome. Don't, I beg you, let the pleasures of Herculaneum keep you from seeing me before you return to Rome.

I have to tell you of our Aunt Gratidia's death, at the age of eighty-five. We had thought her eternal, despite wine and the gout! You know as well as I do that we have lost not only an aunt but a dear dear friend. How much of a friend and benefactor you cannot suspect—even to this day. As I am shortly to give birth to a fifth child and am less strong than I was, I feel the need to say something now which I should have said long ago.

I have before me letters written by Aunt Gratidia. Now that she has gone to join the infernal shades, I intend to destroy one of these letters. I hope you will agree that I do right.

In that letter she confesses to having murdered Lucius Scaurus. She meant him to die much later than he did, thus not involving our family, but she badly misjudged the dose. Gratidia thought to confess when mamma was charged, but so certain were the Scauri of Helvia's guilt that the prosecution would simply have ridiculed the confession as a clumsy attempt by a family member to save her. This would only have made Cicero's task more difficult, and Gratidia was completely confident of his ability to win our case.

Gratidia explains why she killed the man who was my fiancé. A man who deserted before an important battle and was not worthy of being accepted into the family to which she had devoted her life. Then she feared that his habits, which only later she had come to know of, would lead him to abandon or abuse me once he had got my money. You remember that I was to be married *cum manu*. If this had happened, you or our father would have killed him in revenge, and this would almost certainly have led to the ruin of our family. So she acted.

My dear brother, Gratidia's letter is carefully composed and would be judged convincing by most. Perhaps even by our dear mother who to her last day was certain that her own magic spells had been effective. You may not know that when she was dying she sent a large sum of money to the Marsian woman. But now that I too may shortly go down to the underworld, I wish to clear their memories.

One other knew of what Lucius' slaves did to you—an outrageous insult which Gratidia does not mention. One other heard you talk to Gratidia the night before the banquet of the assault made on you. She dissuaded you then from going to Lucius' apartment to kill him by the sword.

O Quintus, I had thought Lucius was a god in disguise. The truth was unbearable. So I did not hesitate—more child than woman as I still was. I saw myself as a tool of Justice. At the banquet I dropped the poison in his goblet as everyone watched the jugglers. Lucius justly cursed his next—and final—throw of dice. For Fate spoke through those dice. And Gratidia—our watchful and wise and loving Gratidia—saw me.

ABOUT THE AUTHOR

Joan O'Hagan is Australian and grew up in Canberra. Since her marriage to an international civil servant she has lived in New Zealand, the South Pacific, America and for many years in Rome. Her interests include Latin and Greek literature, architecture and English poetry. This is her third novel for the Crime Club.